TOGETHER YET
A FOOT APART

GARIMA DAS

Made with ❤ on the Notion Press Platform
www.notionpress.com

Contents

CHAPTER ONE

26th October 2019.

New Delhi

It was 4PM, Mridula, Chavi and Brinda were kneeling on the half-finished big rangoli, drawn in the porch of their duplex house. They were surrounded by packets of colourful rangoli powders, chalk pieces, rangoli stencils and a rag to wipe off any mistakes committed in drawing or filling up of rangoli.

"Mom why don't we put red in the middle and make the petals blue of the small flowers.", suggested little Brinda to her mother while studying the rangoli outline made by Mridula.

"Where have you seen a flower with blue petals, leave alone red center?", taunted her elder sister Chavi. She never missed a chance to show her intelligence over Brinda to ensure her dominance on her.

"O yes, I have! My story book has a lot of them. Besides I love blue.", replied Brinda looking peevishly at her sister before giving a glance at her mother for approval.

"Now don't go on lying just to defend yourself. I am elder to you, so naturally I know better. "

"Not everything. I study everyday with mom in the afternoons. You just waste time on laptop or your new phone which mom has given to you on your last birthday."

'You are a liar. Liar, liar, pants on fire!", Chavi pulled one ponytail of Brinda to rag her.

"No! Don't do that! Ma, look at Chavi, she is teasing me again." Brinda hit Chavi on her arm, who in turn slapped her on her back with more force.

"Oh please! Stop that you two. Can we ever do anything peacefully? You two have come to help me or make my work more difficult?", Mridula scolded them both.

Chavi was now making faces at Brinda, who imitated her to get back at her.

"Why don't you tell her not to call me by my name? She is forgetting her manners. Don't expect me to be nice to her when she can't show some respect to elders. I know she is your favourite amongst the two of us.", snorted Chavi.

This set Mridula thinking, "Had she known the fact she would not be saying this." She bent down and continued the filling up of the rangoli with colours.

"Why are we making the rangoli today itself if Diwali is tomorrow?", asked Brinda. She was more interested in what didi was doing than in the task assigned to her by her mom. She had turned nine last month, which she celebrated by throwing a grand party, just like Chavi's thirteenth birthday party. Her didi was her role model whom she emulated from morning till evening.

"After doing so much of hard work, we want the rangoli to stay for at least 3-4 days of festivities i.e., Choti Diwali, Diwali, Govardhan pooja and Bhai dooj. Moreover, we would be busy tomorrow in preparing sweets, arranging the mandir for puja and lighting Diyas after the Lakshmi Poojan. Now what are you two doing there? I asked Chavi to fill near the outlines and you in the central space, left after didi's fill ups.", clarified Mridula.

She wanted to finish the rangoli before the evening tea so that she could go to the market and be back before the dinner time. She wanted to finish the Diwali shopping that day itself. It was already late by her own standards as she would buy gifts at least a week before the festival. This way she would be ready to reciprocate anyone who paid them a surprise visit for Diwali greetings with Diwali gifts.

Apoorva came out of the house into the porch, "Hey Mridu, how long will you take? I wanted to show you my new sketch. So, you two are also helping mummy? What a pretty rangoli you three have made!" He was very eager to share his latest sketch with Mridula but at the same time didn't want to disturb the lovely mother and daughters' moment together. "No worries, I will wait for you to finish this, then you can give your expert comments on my work." He went inside the house whistling happily.

Chavi stood up, putting her hands on her waist, she sighed, "We must pat our backs for doing a splendid work in such short time. She took out her phone from her pocket and started taking selfies with the rangoli for her Instagram handle. "Mummy I am going with you to the market, isn't it? I want to buy matching earrings with my dress for tomorrow."

"No... I will be taking Brinda though. You stay back as the courier guy is expected to deliver the packet anytime today." They were expecting Diwali gifts from Mridula's brother. "I can get some pretty danglers for you if you want."

"I want to select them myself. All my friends do their own shopping. I am fourteen now, not a kid anymore whose mom does purchasing for her. Besides I can't trust your choice "

"If you don't want me to get it, that's fine by me. But you have to stay back as daddy is busy in his den and dadi has gone out for a walk. I must take Brinda as we need to get her bangles which I can't get without her trying them, as they might not fit her if they are not of the exact size. No such problem with danglers, right?"

"See, I know it for sure that she is your favourite child. You don't love me. You take her with you wherever you go."

Moving forward and holding Chavi in her embrace, Mridula spoke to her softly," What if I told you that it is not true at all. I love both of you equally. I have raised both of you as lovingly."

Brinda, who was observing them with a hint of jealousy in her eyes, out of feeling of being left out, got up and hugged them both. They stood there in threesome embrace for some moments, looking at their handy work, full of satisfaction of a task well done. In that moment, Mridula lost in her past, drifted in deep thoughts. She had come so far after facing so many ups and downs in her life. Last sixteen-seventeen years had been so eventful, so much had transpired, much water had flown under the bridge. In fact, she could sell her story to a producer to make a movie out of it or to a writer maybe to write a novel on it. A smile escaped her lips just thinking about it.

CHAPTER TWO

July of 2000

Indore, Madhya Pradesh

It was early evening, and Mridula had just returned from her college. She immediately went to Gaurav's room, her brother, who was 5 years elder to her. After completing his graduation, he was running a property business in Indore.

She found him sitting on his bed, with their father, Sudeep Goel, who had recently retired from a private job after serving the company for thirty-five years as an Accounts Head. They were enjoying tea and biscuits.

Mridula while helping herself to a biscuit, "You are quite early from office today! What's cooking?"

Sudeep taking a sip of his tea replied, "Having a heart to heart with his father. Any problems?"

"Great! Can I be a part of it too?"

Gaurav winking at her said, "I have finally told him, and the burden is off my chest. He is quite receptive. I was unnecessarily thinking too much about it and was needlessly tense."

"That's what! You should have told him even earlier."

"You both should treat me like your friend now. Mridu, you can confide in me with your secrets, too."

Mridula who had always seen her father only in the mornings and late evenings during his work life, was pleasantly surprised by his mannerisms, "Wow dad, I am sure you have also instructed bhaiya to keep it in control. Ten a day is way too much."

Colour from Gaurav's face started fading, "Mridu...you need rest and something to eat...you must be tired...right?" He was fidgeting now.

"Ten a day? What are you talking about?", Sudeep puzzled.

Mridula realised the blunder she had committed by now, "Tea...cups of tea. I was talking about that."

Sudeep was peering at her, then at Gaurav and again back at her, "No, you didn't mean that. That's two surprises in a day?"

Gaurav blurted out, "She meant that only, tea, coffee. It's quite hectic at work you see."

Sudeep was now snarling, "I have not grown grey without any wisdom, whom are you kidding kiddos? I had a doubt earlier, which is now confirmed." He said to Gaurav, sternly, "Smoking will not only make you grow old sooner, but it will also greatly reduce your stamina. By the way, does your girlfriend, what's her name, Naina knows about this?"

Gaurav to Mridula in frustration, "Yes, have just now told him about her. Thank you dear. You need to improve your cognitive capacity along with your dexterity."

Mridula let out a groan at Gaurav's remark and stomped out of the room.

***

A month later

It was 7AM. The alarm clock was blaring at maximum volume now and was soon going to conk off. Rama Goel, Mridula's mother, entering her room in a huff, shouting at Mridula who was in deep slumber, "Do you want to be late for college yet again? Get up princess!".

"Ten minutes more please ma!", Mridula pulled the bed cover over her head and twisted in her bed.

Rama pulled away the bed cover and tugged at her arm, shook her vigorously to wake her up. Mridula got up cribbing, got dressed for college. She rushed out of the house and strode towards the rickshaw stand.

Mridula's father had a bungalow in Alok Nagar colony in Indore. It was a posh colony with rows of bungalows with garden. It was an old property having three bedrooms, a kitchen and a drawing and dining on the ground floor. It had a big open terrace.

Mridula stopped a few meters before the rickshaw stand, under a tree. She blurted out holding her ears, "Hi! Sorry for being late." She quickly sat pillion on the bike and grabbed Sumit's shoulder with her right hand and the bike's rear with her left. Sumit kick stared the bike, "Don't worry, you know you can rely on my driving skills. We will not miss any class."

MP is the heart of India and Indore in turn is the heart of MP. People are friendly, helpful and simple in here. It was a small town back then which was struggling to become a cosmopolitan with new multinationals trying to come in the market, but at that point in time it typically had only national companies and firms. Traffic was unruly with people parking wherever they liked, not heeding to any traffic rules. Sumit was an expert in these lanes. He could easily meander on his bike through the traffic to reach his destination.

They made it to their college bang on time, just when the bell for the start of the first period went off. Varsha was holding up two empty seats for her friends and was looking in the direction of the classroom door, waiting for her friends to come. They had a pact between them that whoever would reach early would grab the seats for others. She smiled when she saw them sneak inside just behind the teacher, tip toeing into the class.

Preparations were going on in full swing in the college for the upcoming fest. Mridula wanted to participate in the rangoli making and the couples dance competitions being held at the fest. The teacher noting down the details of the students interested in participating in the competitions was sitting on a chair, cramped in between the crowd that thronged her.

"Ahh...excuse me...one minute...excuse please.... aah, yeah. Ma'am, Mridula Goel, B.com second year for rangoli competition.", Sumit held Mridula's hand and made his way through the crowd, pushing and moving diagonally into the gaps as they opened in front of him and called out to the teacher when she became visible. "Sumit and Mridula, B.com second year, for the couples dance competition.", added Mridula.

Varsha was waiting for them, a little away from the crowd. She spoke to them when they returned, "let's check out the sketching competition which is just about to start in the amphitheatre, we have an hour to kill before our English lecture anyway."

They reached the amphitheatre and sat on the wide stairs surrounding the stage. The eleven participants were seated on the stage waiting for the teacher to give them a 'go' signal to start sketching. Each participant had a canvas on a stand in front of him/her. The atmosphere was energetic, and students were busy in all types of activities. Some were hooting, yet some were cheering, few were flying paper planes and were trying to land them on the stage. Mridula, Sumit and Varsha were busy chatting and discussing about the costume for the couple's dance.

After college Sumit dropped Mridula at the turn from where the lane of her house started and turned his motorcycle to go towards his house, which happened to be in the lane adjacent to Mridula's Lane. Mridula checked his muscular stout frame from the back. He wore a purple t-shirt with its sleeves rolled up and ripped blue jeans.

She thought to herself as to why did her mother disapprove of him so strongly. Was it his quirky looks, his not being serious about his studies or the fact that he was not looking for a conventional career in life? He had dreamed of going to America by any means possible, to make it big. He had plans to enter into a decent dancing college in America and get a degree in hip hop dance. His aunt was settled there, who could help him out in finding a good institute. He too wanted to settle there as he saw a bleak chance of making a good career in dancing in India. He wanted a big name for himself and lots of money to lead a comfortable life.

Mridula had known Sumit since eighth grade. That's when he first shifted to Indore from Bangalore and joined her school. She had developed a strong attraction towards him over time, considering his carefree, easy-going attitude for life, apart from the fact that he was a very good dancer. He used to dance in school and college functions, enchanting his audiences with his mesmerising dance moves every time. He too had an affectionate and possessive orientation towards Mridula since school times. He had visited her house a few times on her birthday parties and also on a couple of other occasions, much to the dislike of her parents. Sensing their detest for him, he had stopped going to her house. For the same reason they didn't tell her parents about their going to college together.

They both joined the same college and the same course because they wanted to be in each other's company. Her parents were under the impression that she was commuting to college on a rickshaw whereas she actually went with Sumit on his bike.

She was greeted by Gaurav when she reached home, who was sitting in the drawing room watching news on television. He was hard on hearing as he was hit by a football on his ear when he was in his teens. It had done a permanent injury to his inner ear. Now he wore hearing aids to hear clearly.

"Hi bhaiya! How was your day? Did you take Naina shopping?", Mridula screamed over the Television's volume.

Gaurav was getting married in a month's time. After Sudeep told his wife about their son's affair, she insisted on them getting married shortly afterwards.

Gaurav had met Naina when she came to his office, with her father, as a client. They wanted to sell off their old house and buy a new house in a better locality in Indore.

"Yeah! I am being systematically robbed by her. She liked all the jewellery sets which were way beyond my budget. We did not leave a single jewellery shop in Sarafa bazaar, where we didn't set our foot. Ultimately, I bought her some not so expensive ones, in exchange for treating her to Dahi Bhalla and kachori at Ram Mishthaan Bhandaar."

"Think again while you still have a chance to save yourself. I hope you know what you are getting into. Run away while you can!", she said chuckling and teasing him at the same time. "By the way where is my kachori?"

"What? You were hurt?", replied Gaurav.

"There you go again! I said where is my kachori? Haven't you got it for me? You know I love it!", she repeated in a louder voice for him to hear.

"Oh yeah, I have! Go take it from the kitchen slab, next to the mixer."

"I knew you would.", Mridula giggled with delight and paced towards the kitchen.

Her mother who was rolling chapatis in the kitchen, without looking up, "So, you are back? How are your studies going?"

"Okay okay, …. yummy, munch..munch...", Mridula replied to her mother and stuffed a kachori in her mouth at the same time.

"What do you plan to do after B.com?"

"Not thought about it yet."

"I have. I want you to get married and settle down in life on time. It's always good for girls to have babies in their early twenties. Late marriage, then late childbirth, leads to a lot of health complications in women. Rajni aunty's nephew is a handsome boy drawing fat salary in Bangalore. He is working with some IT company and doing very well for himself. Should I..... "

"No, please no!"

"And why not?"

"Please don't bully me like you did bhaiya."

"Don't you want to marry and have a family of your own?"

"Not so early ma. Not before three, or four years at least."

Rama shook her head in frustration. It was not that Mridula had not thought about getting married or was averse to the idea of marriage, but it was more to do with marrying an unknown guy. "How could one give oneself completely to a stranger and be committed for life", she often thought. She always dreamt of having a husband who was her friend first and anything else later. She wanted a partner who would encourage her to be much more than just his wife and support her in every aspect of life, rather than confining her to the kitchen and kids or constantly kept demanding and directing her. An ideal partner would consult his wife before taking major decisions in life. She had seen her father and mother as an ideal couple since childhood but lately she had started noticing flaws even in their relationship. She didn't like the way her father bossed over her mother or considered his word as the final verdict in any matter. To compensate for her non-involvement in important matters, especially financial, her mother had donned a stubborn personality wherever she had a little say.

Mridula wanted a life partner who would treat her as his equal in every matter or situation that life might throw; a partner who would not be afraid of exploring and learning with her; and definitely would not consider it below his dignity to consult his wife in important life decisions.

***

A few days later

Sumit and Mridula were waiting in the green room. They were expected to be called on to the stage anytime soon, for their Salsa dance performance. They had been practicing in free time between lectures since a month now. Varsha was sitting in the audience with Ahmad and ten to fifteen other classmates to cheer for them. Their names were called on the stage. Sumit held Mridula's hand firmly and gave her a reassuring look that all would be fine, "Breathe, take a deep breath and exhale loudly. Come...". He led her to the stage, and they stood facing each other.

Sumit's right hand went on her waist and the left hand held her right hand just above the shoulder level. Their music started. They started their dance and audience started cheering. Mridula gave it her all. By the end of their performance, they both were out of breath. The stage was on fire with everyone cheering and shouting their names.

They stood third in the competition. Mridula was visibly upset as she held herself responsible for not getting the first position for them, "I am sure they could make out my fumbling despite you covering it up with finesse. I am sorry, you deserve a better dance partner.", she uttered.

"Don't be stupid! If it was not perfect, it wasn't that bad either. You gave your best performance. That's all that matters."

Varsha intervening, "Yeah! You guys were the best! The judges were partial towards the MTI college's group. I think one of the judges was from that college, so he favoured them."

"In fact, we should go for a picnic to celebrate our victory.", added Sumit.

"Let's go to Tincha falls. It is beautiful during monsoon times", exclaimed Varsha all excited.

"Fine then, Ahmed and I will pick you two up this Saturday morning, in his car. How about 10AM?", Sumit said, firming up the program.

Before Mridula could say anything, Varsha blurted out, "Done, we will be ready by 10AM. We can tell our parents that we are going to the library to study. We must tell the same thing to our parents so that in case they talk to each other, our lie is not caught."

***

Saturday morning

All four of them were driving towards Tincha falls, in Ahmad's Maruti 800. He had recently learned driving and got the driving licence only a month back. It took him around one and a half hours to cover the 30 kms of distance, as he was driving slowly and carefully, in order not to cause any damage to his father's car. By the time they reached the falls, it was already nearing lunch time. They grabbed the roasted corn on the cob from a hawker sitting there and stood near the railing, watching the mesmerising waterfall.

Sumit was noticing Mridula's petite figure, which looked even more delicate in a pink suit she wore that day. She paired it with a pink Bindi and pink bangles. She had clipped her hair on the sides and left her long hair open at the back. She was stylish and had a radiant personality and always smelled incredible. Her body was shapely. Her big black eyes seemed to be searching for something meaningful, almost as if like desiring to live a full and rich life. Sumit immediately looked away the moment Mridula sensed him gazing at her at length and in response she gave him an abashed look.

In the windy weather, she was finding it tedious to eat her corn along with trying to manage her long hair and dupatta, which were uncontrollably flying in all directions. She was looking even more beautiful than her usual self. He had come determined that day to tell her his feelings, but he was finding it difficult to concentrate on what he would say, as he was distracted by her charm and her ordeal with the wind. He mustered some courage and spoke to her, "Here, let me hold your bhutta while you tie your hair with your dupatta."

"Good idea Mridula. You know what, you should have worn trousers instead like Varsha. It gets quite windy out here sometimes.", said Ahmad. Mridula gave her bhutta to Sumit to hold and started to tie her hair with the dupatta. Sensing something brewing between them, he got better sense to leave the two of them alone and so he spoke to Varsha, "Look at those Monkeys there Varsha. Would you like to feed them peanuts? We can buy some there." He took Varsha away. Sumit liked his move and thanked him in his head.

While she tied her hair, Sumit cleared his throat and finally blurted out to Mridula, "You are looking very beautiful in this pink suit."

"Really? Thanks.", she said taking her bhutta back from him.

"Not only today, but you always look beautiful. I mean, ...I find you extremely pretty. "

She paused her eating to look at him over her corn on the cob. Awkward silence followed for a couple of moments.

"I will come to the point; I want you to be my girlfriend. "

"What....I am your girlfriend. Am I not?"

"Not like that. I mean serious relationship, commitment, ... you know what I mean."

"No... not really. What do you mean Sumit?"

"Okay, if you want to hear it clearly, I want us to commit to each other. May be even marry each other later in life. Now do you get me?"

"I..hmmm...you mean...see, you know I like you, right. Otherwise, why would I be here with you after lying to my parents about my whereabouts. I feel a sense of hygge with you which I cannot deny."

"Oh! I am so glad to hear that!"

"But I don't get the commitment part."

"Why not, what's wrong in that?"

"What's the hurry? We are not running away anywhere. We are so young; we will meet other people in life; there is so much more to explore still. How can we make up our mind at this point."

Sumit wanted to counter her but instead spoke, "Here they come. We will talk some other time, okay?"

They first dropped back Varsha and then Mridula.

When Mridula entered her house, her mother entered behind her.

"You are studying very hard this time. I am sure you will really do well in the exams.", she taunted her.

"Yes mummy. I am trying."

"When did you start lying to me? I thought you told me everything. Don't you feel ashamed of yourself? You are well aware that papa and I do not like that guy, still you..."

"Huh! I don't get you. What are you talking?"

"Oh, come on! Cut that out. I saw you stepping out of that car. That boy, what's his name, Sumit was sitting in the front. Where were you the whole day?"

"I don't want to lie to you. I am sorry! Please don't tell papa. We had gone to Tincha."

"See Mridu! I think that he is not a very sincere boy. As far as doing friendship is concerned, I don't mind, but please, don't do anything beyond that. Please don't get involved emotionally. That boy doesn't have a future! We have a status in Indore. For God's sake don't destroy it. What does he plan to do in life? When will he get settled? We don't know, right? His family background is also not very sound. We will find a good match for you. We want you to be happy in life."

"Mom, I am not thinking along those lines yet. He is just a good friend, nothing more, rest assured."

Rama raising her voice," Do you think that any decent guy will marry you after you roam around with him like this?"

"Times have changed ma. People are not that narrow minded now as they were when you were young. It's twenty first century."

"Don't give me that shit! When it comes to marrying a girl, all boys are conservative, at least in India. I want this to end here as I don't want you barking up the wrong tree, otherwise, I will have to tell papa."

Mridula wanted to add, she wanted to say that it was only her mother's belief. Believes are not facts and are often based on imagination and insecurities. No one can ever predict one's own future, leave alone others. She kept quiet instead as she knew there was no point arguing when she herself was not sure of committing to Sumit. Why waste her energy on something which was not significant at that point? She could, infact, talk about it in future, if she became interested in him or when the right time came.

CHAPTER THREE

Early 2001

Mridula, Varsha, Sumit and Ahmad, were coming out of the class after the Accounts lecture. Ahmad to the group, "I am in a mood for an ice cream. Who wants to have one?"

"I don't mind one. We can gorge on the aloo parathas which Mridula has got before that", said Sumit winking at Varsha. "All these balance sheets and ledgers have made me really hungry."

"Why is it so crowded in the library? Let's check it out guys.", Mridula started walking towards the library. The gang followed her.

The results of the sketching competition from the fest were being showcased in the library on popular demand from students. All the sketches were displayed on the walls of the library for everyone to see. They started to check out the sketches and comment on each one of them.

Sumit was standing in front of the sketch which had won the first prize, "The umbrella is too large for the man."

"He has just returned from playing golf and is carrying a golf umbrella.", said Varsha and everyone laughed.

Mridula was looking at the sketch which stood second, "This is a better one. He should have got the first prize."

Varsha was looking at a sketch of a lady, "This is an attractive young woman here. Why do I feel like I have seen her somewhere?"

"Because she looks like Mridula! See the eyes, the nose, quite like her.", pointed out Ahmad.

Sumit came closer to the board to get a clearer view, "It is Mridula, no doubt about it. Even her earrings are the same. Who is the artist?". Tilting his head to read the name, "Apoorva Verma, LLB, final year.

***

About a week later

Mridula and Varsha were standing at the stationery shop in college. Varsha was interacting with the shopkeeper, "I want a blue and a black gel pen. Give a thick register also. Not this, thicker. How much?"

Mridula was standing a little away from the counter lost in her thoughts. She noticed a fair, lean and a tall guy, who coming in her direction, from her right side. When he came nearer, she noticed that he had a smile on his face as if he knew her. She was perplexed and tried to remember whether she knew the guy? Before she could place him, he spoke up, "Hi! So good to see you here."

"Do I know you? Sorry I...", she uttered with puzzled and perplexed look on her face.

"You have even bigger, black and such clear eyes up close. One can easily get lost in their depth. Had I seen you from this close I would have sketched just your eyes."

Mridula tried to speak something but blurted out just some gibberish. She was unable to think or speak clearly, as she was bewildered by the stranger, "What? Who...Ohh...you are...", ultimately realisation seeped into her, "are you Apoorva?"

Apoorva was smiling, "Yes, so you are sharp as well."

Mridula's face flushed in red, and she suddenly became very self-conscious. She started looking in the direction of her friend as a refuge because she could no longer look him in the eye. Apoorva realising her state, spoke, "Didn't mean to make you uncomfortable. I would definitely like to meet you sometime at leisure, to know you better."

In the meanwhile, Varsha had finished her stationery purchase and joined her friend. She looked quizzingly at the person standing next to her, engaged in conversation. She nevertheless greeted him and asked Mridula, "Won't you introduce me?"

Mridula now taking a hold of herself spoke, "Yeah! Varsha he is Apoorva, Apoorva this is Varsha."

Varsha's eyes widened, "The Apoorva? Who...ok. Nice to meet you, finally! By the way you sketch really well. I feel that you should have been placed in one of the top three positions."

"Yes, you have a good hand.", blurted Mridula.

"Thanks for the compliments but the credit goes more to the muse. I couldn't resist myself when I saw her that day sitting in the amphitheatre. I had to sketch her."

Varsha, amused, looked from Apoorva to Mridula and back to Apoorva. The sound of 'uuuhhh' escaped her lips.

"Please stop that. You are exaggerating.", said Mridula fidgeting and shifting from one foot to the other.

"Okay! Point taken. Now tell me, when are we meeting again?"

"I don't know. I can't say."

Varsha disappointed by her reply, "what? Exchange numbers and fix up something. By the way we are getting late for our Mercantile Law class, you write down her number, 4...5...9........"

***

About a month later

It was early evening. Mridula was in her room, sewing a matching scarf with her skirt. She wanted to pursue textile designing after B.com. Her imagination took off when she touched the fabric.

In the drawing room her father and brother were sitting and chit chatting. Rama was in the kitchen preparing dinner and cribbing loudly, "I thought that I will get some respite from kitchen work once Gaurav's bride came home. But no, maharaniji will not peep into the kitchen unless and until asked to, specifically."

The landline in the drawing room rang. Sudeep Goel got up to answer it.

"Hello....Hello.... HEELLOOO......"

Gaurav told his father, "leave it papa. No one is speaking. Probably a wrong number. I also picked up a blank call some 10 minutes back."

Later in the evening the phone rang again. This time it was picked up by Mridula. She peeked in the corridor leading from drawing room to the bedrooms. Assessing and ensuring that no one was within the hearing range, she started to speak, "Hello, hi! Yeah, all good. You tell."

Apoorva was complaining to her about ignoring him in the college, "why did you ignore me? I kept waving at you."

"Actually, Sumit wouldn't have been comfortable with me talking to you, so..."

"Why in the God's name should you even bother about what he thinks? If you want to speak to me, you don't need his approval. Or do you?"

"I don't, but.... he is a very old friend and extremely possessive of me"

"See, I talk to you over the phone, that's fine, but I would like to meet you in person as well."

"How is it possible in the college?"

"We can meet outside of college. If you try, it is possible."

"Ok, tomorrow let's meet at Rajwada Palace. Will that be fine by you?"

"That would be lovely. But you come alone. Reach around 3PM. Wait for me near the ticket counter."

"Ok. Done then. See you tomorrow."

***

Next day

Apoorva was checking his watch for the umpteenth time. He was shunting in front of the Rajwada gate with a chip on his shoulder. He was visibly upset about her being late. The eagerness to meet her and chat with her face to face, was killing him. When he looked up, he spotted her getting out of a rickshaw.

"You are twenty minutes late.", Apoorva blurted out the moment he saw her.

Mridula while taking out change from her purse and counting it, "The khajoori Bazaar was so damn crowded. Took us quite a while to cross it."

"Oh yeah! And I landed from a helicopter." She looked at him and rolled her eyes.

Apoorva had already bought the tickets. They proceeded inside the Palace through the huge wooden door at the entrance. The majestic seven story building made out of wood, stone and marble, some two hundred years ago, looked attractive. Its sheer grandeur was overwhelming. They crossed the front courtyard to enter the galleried rooms, passed souvenir shop, mandir and fountains, chatting all the while and praising its splendour.

An hour had passed since they arrived. Mridula expressed her exhaustion from all the walking in the heat, "I am tired, and my feet are also hurting in these heels."

"Remove your heels and give them to me. Here, you can wear my sandals.", said Apoorva removing his sandals.

"No way!"

There was no one nearby or in sight. Apoorva held her hand and cornered Mridula against a wall. He kept both his hands on the wall encasing her between himself and the wall. Both faced each other. He was looking down, straight into her eyes. She was five feet and five inches, which is not short by a girl's standard. But against Apoorva, who was six feet and one inch, she had to strain her neck to look him in the eye.

Apoorva spoke in a soft tone, "Your eyes are so clear. They say that the eyes are the window to one's soul. Jet black, and so deep!" He took a deep long breath and exhaled with a sound, "Huh! You know, I have started liking you a lot. I love to talk to you over the phone so much that I can do so for hours, without getting tired." And then he bent over to touch her lips with his and pulled her closer to himself, with one hand around her waist. She resisted for a moment but then gave in. She was surprised by herself when her hand slowly moved to hold the front of his shirt. Apoorva now held her in both his arms, pushing his body against her. His body pressed against her as one of his hands moved to caress her flowing hair. He held her in his embrace for some time and then released her quickly when he heard some footsteps approaching towards them.

They hastily left that spot, came out of the palace in awkward silence. They stood on the street avoiding eye contact and looked away in search of any appropriate words to say. Ultimately Apoorva broke the silence, "I will call you after an hour, at about 5:30PM. Ensure that you pick it up. Bye then."

CHAPTER FOUR

Summer of 2002

A year had passed since Mridula and Apoorva were seeing each other. Mridula was now in Third year of B.com. Apoorva had joined some other college to pursue master's in law. He planned to join a law firm in Delhi after his masters.

They talked to each other over the phone every day and met on the weekends. She slowly grew away from Sumit. She felt closer to Apoorva than Sumit, when she compared them both. She felt a contrast in Sumit's pomposity against Apoorva's modesty, dreamy vagueness of Sumit against Apoorva's surety of decisiveness. The fact that her parents disapproved of Sumit also had a role to play in her moving away from him and getting drawn towards Apoorva.

It was Sunday afternoon. Apoorva, Mridula and Varsha were sitting at a small cafe. They were devouring the chocolate pastries and coffee. Mridula lifted her gaze from the chocolate tart to look outside the window. She noticed two men in grey safari suits, standing near a Pan shop under the tree; who in turn were looking in their direction. They turned their gaze elsewhere when they noticed Mridula looking at them.

Mridula whispered to Apoorva, "I don't mean to scare you, but we are being followed around the town."

"What? What are you saying?", Varsha almost choked on the cold coffee. She followed Mridula's gaze to look at the two men.

"Really? Are you sure?", Apoorva casually looking in the direction of the men.

Mridula in a very serious tone, "Yes, of course! I have noticed these two men following us a couple of times earlier too. But the question is who would spy on us and why would they spy on us?"

"Could be your brother's spies. He must have kept them to spy on you after your mother told him that you are very pally with Sumit", concluded Varsha.

"Quite a possibility!", Apoorva looked towards the two men at the pan shop. He glanced at Mridula who was looking tense and was nervously tracing the rim of the coffee mug with her finger, lost in thought. He could not hold it any longer and burst out laughing, "Relax dear. They are here for me and not for you."

Varsha and Mridula stared at Apoorva in disbelief.

"Yes, they are! My father is an Additional Collector, Indore. He is concerned about my security. So, he has appointed them for me. They are always around me. If you have not noticed them then they are doing a very good job. Pretty soon he would be retiring, so, all this circus is going to end. Thankfully."

Mridula let out a sigh of relief. Varsha snickered under her breath.

***

A Few days later

Mridula hurried to the drawing room to answer the phone when she heard it ringing. She picked up the phone, "Hello! Yeah, I am fine. No, I wanted to study at home only." She was expecting Apoorva's call but instead it was

Sumit's.

Sumit had called to ask her if she was interested in joint studies in college library, for the exams which were due in a months' time. He was complaining to her, "You no longer go to college with me, at least we can study together. You can guide me wherever I have doubts."

"Going to college and coming back takes a lot of time. Since colleges are closed now, there is no point wasting time in going there. You carry on if you want. Ask Varsha or Ahmed to accompany you if they like. They might be interested. What is the progress on your going to America?"

"Hmmm. Visa is en route and will arrive soon. I will be going immediately after the exams. My aunt has arranged my admission with one of the top institutes of California."

"I am so happy for you. I know you will reach great heights in whatever you do."

"I wanted to say something, if you don't mind."

"Sumit, since when have you started thinking so much before talking to me?"

"I don't like the way you have distanced yourself from me after you have become close to that Apoorva. We used to be so close. I miss that, yes, I do. I know that now I would be leaving for America. When or if I return, is a question mark, but this equation between us is something I never thought would ever arise. You take care and always remember that you have a very special place in my heart, always."

Mridula didn't know what to say to that and after some moments of silence spoke, "I know that, Sumit. Please know that you too have a very special place in my heart. No one can take that place which you hold, but I don't know what else to say?"

"Hmmm. Chalo bye. Gotta go.", he sensed that she didn't want to continue the conversation.

"Bye!", said Mridula.

As Mridula turned to go towards her room, she heard muffled sounds. She tried to make out where were they coming from. She realised they were coming from Gaurav's room. It sounded like Naina was crying. She stopped and stood there for a couple of minutes to make sure. When the sobbing didn't stop, she slowly opened the room door to peep inside.

Naina was sitting on the edge of the bed with her face buried in her palms. She was startled by the sound of the door opening. She was not expecting company in her room. She looked towards Mridula with wet eyes and red face, "oh! I thought you were studying in your room. Some smoke went into my eyes while cooking. I was just going back to the kitchen."

"What happened?", asked Mridula concerned. She bent down to hug her sympathetically.

From all the empathy, Naina couldn't control her tears and burst out crying loudly. She embraced Mridula for comfort, who was holding her face in her hands, gently pushing it upwards, to look into her eyes.

"If you won't tell me, I am going to feel really bad."

Naina controlled her sobbing and spoke in a cracked, broken voice, "She doesn't like whatever I do. She has told me to use less oil in cooking. Today I had done the same in 'Upma'. Now she is complaining that the onions were not properly fried which spoiled the taste. When I use less oil, onions will not taste the same, right? For her I don't seem to be doing anything right."

"But she is the same with everybody. Don't you think? She has a dry sense of cynicism but that doesn't mean that she is against you or doesn't like you. Don't worry, I will speak with her."

"No no, you don't tell her anything."

"Okay, as you say. But now I want you to wash your face and give me a smile. A fake one will also do. Aren't you getting late for boutique?

"Hmmm."

Mridula pulled her to a standing position, "Come on, get ready!"

***

Yet a few days later

Mridula was on the terrace, listening to her favourite songs, lost in thoughts of Apoorva. She found him endearingly cute. Once he got her chocolates, but she refused to take them, claiming that they would cause her to gain weight and cause pimples on her face. To which he replied that he wouldn't mind her face full of pimples or she being fat. He accepted her as she was.

She came out of her daydreaming when her bhabhi came rushing to the terrace, all hysterical and teary eyed.

"What's the matter Naina?"

"Gaurav just called; he is surrounded by some goons. They are carrying knives.... I am....what do I do....", she was overcome with emotions and burst out crying."

"Control yourself and tell me how you know this?"

"He called up. Papa just talked to him and has immediately rushed to his office. What can we do?"

Mridula's brain was running fast. She thought about Apoorva and ran downstairs to call him up for help. She was certain that he would definitely be able to help with his resources.

When she reached the drawing room, she could hear her mother mumbling and weeping in her room. She grabbed the land line and started dialling his number.

"Hi! I don't know what you can do but I could think of no one else. My brother is in trouble... armed men have entered his office.... yeah, note down the address.... it's 31/B2, shopping complex, ..."

"Don't worry, it will be taken care of.", Apoorva assured her in a calm voice.

In about a couple of hours, which seemed like an eternity, the doorbell rang. Naina quickly opened the door. Sudeep and Gaurav Goel entered the house. Gaurav was visibly shaken. Sudeep was tense. Everyone waited in silence for them to speak.

Finally, Sudeep spoke, "We were saved at the nick of time today by God sent men. They were armed and were wearing safari suits. They took charge and handled the situation very maturely. Now Gaurav will tell who the goons were and how did the matter reach this far."

Gaurav cleared his throat and collected himself to speak in a broken voice "They were Munna bhaiya's men. I have purchased some land from him. There was some confusion about the payment. I told him an amount but over the phone he was insisting for a greater amount. That day was very busy, and clients were sitting with me. I was unable to concentrate on both or maybe there was a lapse in my hearing."

Rama interrupted him, "Why did they come with knives?"

"Will you let him finish before you ask questions?", scolded Sudeep.

"I sent him the amount which I thought we had agreed upon, through an office boy. Receiving that amount, he started insisting on the amount which he had been expecting and the matter just escalated. He was not ready to listen and....."

"I am still wondering who the men in safari suits were? How did they reach your shop? How...", Sudeep uttered perplexed.

Mridula spoke cutting him midway, "I can answer these questions. My friend Apoorva is a son of an IAS officer. I called and asked him for help when bhabhi narrated me the whole scenario."

All heads turned towards Mridula, and she continued, "I think I should call him up to thank him for his timely help."

"Friend from where? I mean how do you know him? You never mentioned him before.", enquired Rama.

Mridula was contemplating about what and how much to say. She tried to speak after quietening the commotion in her head, "He was in my college only. He is now pursuing master's in law from some other college. We kept in touch after he left my college."

"Is he a special friend or just an acquaintance?", queried Gaurav, who had now normalised.

Rama jumping in, "Do you think an acquaintance will send men for helping her brother?"

"Is he good looking?", asked Naina in a muffled voice. Rama immediately shot a contemptuous look at Naina.

"He seems to be a nice guy. Call him on dinner tomorrow. I would like to meet him.", Sudeep instructed Mridula.

CHAPTER FIVE

Early 2003

Parents of both Apoorva and Mridula had approved of their match and had made up their minds for their wedding to take place in near future.

Mridula, Gaurav and Naina were to meet Apoorva in a restaurant that day, to talk about how things would work out for the marriage, once Apoorva moved to Delhi for work. He was completing final year of his master's that summer. When Sudeep Goel came to know about Apoorva's moving to Delhi shortly, he grew apprehensive for Mridula and asked his son to formally discuss in detail with Apoorva, about how they will make arrangements for marriage, being in two different cities.

Naina came out of her room, "I am ready to go. I think we should leave now without any further delay. I have taken half a day off. Can't shut the boutique for the whole day."

Rama glanced at Naina from head to toe, "You will go like this? Can't you wear anything decent. You are not a schoolgirl to wear a skirt."

"What's wrong with a skirt? Mridu wears it too."

"Gaurav beta, would you like your wife to go to the restaurant like this? I know she is a designer, but this is just not an appropriate attire for the occasion. What will people think, what will Apoorva think of our family?"

Gaurav shook his head, "Ma, let her. If she likes it, I'm fine with it."

Rama felt offended when her son took his wife's side, "If you can't control her, then someone has to speak. I don't know what magic has she done on you. You don't see any fault of hers, ever!"

Gaurav while shaking his head, "What nonsense do you speak?"

Sudeep Goel tried to terminate the swordplay between the mother and the son. He said to Mridula, who had just entered the drawing room, "Mridu when will you be completing your textile designing course?"

"In about 2-3 months' time. Why do you ask pa?"

"Do you plan to work after that, or should we plan your marriage soon after? I think you should get married. You can start working after marriage in Delhi."

Gaurav intervened for his little sis, "We are not in a hurry to send her away. Let her find her niche, let her take time to prepare herself mentally for the responsibilities that come with married life. What say Mridu?"

Mridula smiling at her brother, then addressing her father, "I want to join a textile company after completing the course. In fact, my teacher would be helping me in finding a suitable opening. Marriage cannot happen before at least a year."

"Hmmm, okay, I am happy to hear that you are not limiting your options in your eagerness to marry him. After getting some experience here, I am sure you will get immense opportunities in Delhi, once you move in with him. Keep this point in mind too while discussing with Apoorva."

***

July ,2003

By the time monsoons came both Apoorva and Mridula had completed their respective courses. Mridula came to know through Varsha that Sumit had left for US a month back. A part of her was sad and wondered whether she would ever see him again. Somewhere inside she felt a little bit guilty for ignoring him after meeting and knowing Apoorva. She wanted him to succeed in life and secretly prayed for him in her heart. She felt bad that things had so developed between them that he didn't even give her a call before going.

She was meeting Apoorva for the last time before he went to Delhi. They were sitting on a bench in a park. Her hand was in his hand, and they were looking at each other. Apoorva was speaking very softly, almost whispering, "We will be in touch. I will buy a mobile phone and a sim card as soon as I reach Delhi. You too buy one here. We can talk privately, without the fear of others listening to us."

"I will try, if dad allows, that is. Maybe I will persuade bhaiya to gift me one or I will have to wait till my first salary comes. It is quite expensive you see."

"In that case, I will buy you one and send it by courier."

"They will not like that too. We will work out something, don't worry."

Apoorva removing a stray strand of hair from her forehead, "I cannot promise you a bed of roses Mridu, but I promise you my unconditional love and my heart."

She put her head on his shoulder, and they sat there for some time before bidding goodbye to each other, with heavy hearts.

CHAPTER SIX

New Delhi

Late 2004

Mridula and Apoorva were married for some months now. They stayed with Apoorva's parents, Rajendra and Seema Verma, in their bungalow. Apoorva had started working under a Delhi high court advocate. Mridula had left work in Indore. Now she was spending her time as a house maker and was on the lookout to join a textile designer or some textile firm in Delhi. She resigned from her job in Indore at the time of her marriage. Rajendra Verma's health hadn't been keeping very well lately. He had high sugar and blood pressure, for which he had to take medication; so, he was very particular about his diet. After his retirement from job, his family had started staying in their old bungalow in South Delhi.

It was a duplex house. On the ground floor, there was a kitchen, a drawing-dining, a bedroom with attached washroom, which was occupied by Apoorva's parents and another small guest bedroom with attached washroom. On the first floor there were two rooms with attached washrooms. One of them was Apoorva's bedroom and the other was his study, which he often referred to as 'the den'. The house help had a shed and a small toilet in the garden area of the bungalow. There was a garage, used as a car park and a porch in front of the house. The house had a beautiful garden in the back side, with lawn and flowers. Both the rooms on the first floor had a separate balcony each.

Despite having a full-time house help, Ravi, Mridula still kept busy with the household work for the entire day. She tried to learn the mannerism and the ways of the new house and tried hard to please everyone. Everything was new for her; she was used to be served but now she served everyone else before herself. She had started putting alarm to wake up at a decent time so that she could freshen up before being ready with the breakfast for everyone. She was trying to remember that her father-in-law liked a crisp chapati whereas mother-in-law preferred it soft. She now knew that her in laws liked simple chaunk(tempering) in dal and sabzi whereas Apoorva liked masala of onion and garlic in his dishes. Rajendra liked food piping hot, but Apoorva wanted just warm enough. She had literally forgotten what she liked or couldn't care the least. She ate whatever was conveniently available or no one else ate as she didn't like to waste food plus, she didn't want to make any efforts for herself after she had already done enough for others.

She saw to it that the house was at least neat if not spick and span. She had learned to note down things, made a list of items which were to be replenished in the house and things to be repaired or changed. She went for shopping for the provisions, vegetables and fruits. All this was earlier done by Seema. Now that Mridula had come, she spent more time with Rajendra, who was becoming laxed in taking care of himself. Seema would help out Mridula if she asked for but would not do things on her own accord.

Sometimes Mridula took her mother-in-law and father-in-law to their relative's house or to their doctors', as she knew driving. Basically, her whole day went in household chores. Apoorva, on the other hand, desired her undivided attention and pampering whenever he was at home.

That day she was not feeling completely fit. She felt giddy while coming down the stairs. She was worried as her periods were overdue. She had asked Apoorva to get her a pregnancy test kit while coming back from work.

She sat on the toilet seat the next morning and took a hard look at the pregnancy test strip. It looked like two lines alright. She was still doubtful, so, she carried the strip to show to Apoorva, who was still in bed, sleeping.

"Listen, do you think it is positive?"

"What? Shut your mouth and let me sleep. Why are you waking me up? Are you out of your mind? I am tired. Don't you know I have a hard and busy day ahead. Smallest of things you can't do yourself."

She was hurt by his reaction. She expected him to be a little more concerned. She was noticing a different side of him after marriage. This Apoorva was detached from her vis a vis the one whom she had met at the bookstore.

"Can you get another kit today. I want to be sure."

"Can't you wait till I wake up? Impatient lady."

"Sorry, but I too wake up early irrespective of what time I sleep dear.", she retorted annoyed.

"Now you want to argue like a fool and wake me up."

"I am just...."

"Just shut up! Shhh...Will you?", Apoorva said in a raised voice.

He changed side and went to sleep again. She was further disturbed by his behaviour and lack of concern.

In the evening when Apoorva got her another kit, she didn't take it to show her anger on his behaviour in the morning. Apoorva came after her to cajole her.

"What is the matter? Take it, that's what you asked for."

"I am not feeling good. Have you forgotten what happened in the morning?"

"Ohh come on! I was sleeping and you were disturbing me. Then you argued."

"I was so upset by your behaviour that I couldn't eat the whole day."

"I am so sorry. See I am touching my ears. Now go and use it. We should be sure."

Mridula came out of the bathroom, holding the strip in one hand.

Apoorva curiously, "Yes, what is it?"

Mridula shook her head up and down, gauging his reaction. Apoorva came next to her and lifted her in the air and started laughing madly.

***

Couple of months later

Mridula was in the kitchen making chapatis for dinner. Apoorva, Rajendra and Seema, were sitting on the dining table, awaiting dinner. She had slowed down since her pregnancy had been confirmed. Although she was happy about it but somewhere inside, she was sad that she wouldn't be able to join a job immediately, as her health was not at its best. She felt very lonely and lost after her marriage.

Seema said in frustration to Rajendra, "It's already late for your medicines. When will she get the chapatis?" She blurted out loud, "How long will you take? The dal and vegetable are getting cold."

Rushing out of the kitchen with a plate of chapatis, Mridula started serving them.

"Tasteless! I can't eat this. Dal is just boiled water.", Apoorva commented and pushed his plate aside.

Rajendra took a bite and made an unpleasant face. He looked at Mridula and then towards Apoorva, "Appu beta, order something for yourself. While you are doing that, order some sweet for me too. I Really need it to better my taste after eating this garbage."

Mridula went back to the kitchen and stood there staring at the gas stove, fighting back her tears. She couldn't help but remember how Rajendra had got samosas from the market a few days back. When she took out one from the packet to eat, Rajendra immediately told her not to finish them all and to save some for Apoorva, too, simultaneously commenting that they were his favourite. He never asked or cared whether they were her favourite too. Not that she wanted to eat them all or wouldn't have kept his share. She missed being pampered, taken care off, feeling important and belonged in the house. She felt that she received a bad bargain in the marriage. She felt like an outsider in the house. Despite trying her best to fit in, to win everyone's heart, still something or the other went wrong repeatedly.

She wiped a tear that escaped her left eye before Ravi, who was standing near the sink doing dishes, noticing it. She swallowed hard and controlled the rest of her tears. It had taken her one and a half hours to make the dinner which no one liked. Before marriage she had never bothered to enter the kitchen other than the times when her mother was unwell. Just like Apoorva she too was busy with studies and later with her job. Yet after marriage she was expected to be an expert in culinary art whereas Apoorva got to sit and comment on her hard work. How was this fair from any angle, she wondered?

Seema entered the kitchen, "If you can't cook, tell me, I will do it." Her tone was loud enough to reach the dining area.

Apoorva yelled from his seat, "If you have to do it mummy then what will she do? I don't want you to stand in the kitchen at this age. Keep a cook instead."

It was very easy for Mridula to keep a cook and say that she couldn't cook to escape all the criticism. But she wanted to take responsibility of her house and cook for her family. Only if everyone in the house had been a little more understanding and patient with her, she could learn everything in no time.

***

Early 2005

Standing in front of the mirror one morning, Mridula was combing her hair. She looked at her eight months pregnant body's reflection in the mirror. Looking blankly at herself, she was lost in thoughts, "Apoorva seems to be so distant and unapproachable now, in contrast to his patient, caring and loving self before marriage. I had never seen him angry or misbehave before. He often sleeps in his study room on the pretext of working late at night. But he is either reading late into the night or is on his phone. What could be the reason for his changed behaviour? Am I not good enough for him? Am I not as per his expectations from his life partner? I am making a lot of efforts in this relationship, but still...."

Her mobile phone rang, shaking her out of her train of thoughts. She checked the screen to see who was calling her. It was Varsha.

She picked up the phone, "Hello!"

"Hi Mridu! How are you dear?"

"Varsha, so good to hear from you! I am ok. What about you?"

"Only 'ok'? You must be on cloud nine. Aunty told me about your pregnancy when I went to your place today.

Congratulations sweetheart."

"Thanks! And what's up with you? How come you went to mom's place?"

"I am getting married! Went to give the card to your parents."

"Really? Who is the unlucky one?", Mridula tried to crack a joke to lighten up her mood.

"Yeah! His name is Siddharth. He is from Mumbai. I will be moving there after marriage. You tell, how is everything? You have forgotten all about me since your marriage."

"What should I tell? Life is busy with routine housework, which is getting more and more difficult to do now because of my condition. I tell you, don't be in a hurry to conceive after marriage, take precautions till you feel that you both are ready to take on the responsibility."

"I know. He he …. Listen, I wanted to tell you something you know. I met Naina at your place. She, sort of gave me a hint that they would not be staying with your parents for long. Gaurav bhaiya is getting a flat ready and most probably they would be moving out before monsoon."

Mridula was again lost in thoughts, "Nothing seems to be going right in life. I should call bhaiya to ask him to speak to mom, before taking such a big step. He can make her understand that she needs to tone it down. She should treat her daughter-in-law as her daughter and be patient in teaching her the ways of the house. Teach her some, learn from her sometimes. She is not an illiterate or a child. She too has some competence and is not a complete nincompoop in life, as mom treats her to be. Only then will Naina feel at home and appreciated in life, which in turn will make her give her two hundred percent to the family. Why don't people understand this simple fact. Only when daughter-in-law is treated like a daughter, will she be able to adopt the house as her own."

"Hellooo.., anybody home?", blared Varsha on the speaker.

"Yeah yeah, very much here. You tell, have you started shopping for the big day? How I wish I was there."

"Come to the wedding. I will miss you otherwise."

"Yeah, right! Huh! How I wish I could."

"Mridu, you don't sound yourself. Everything is ok, right?"

"Life after marriage is not like how we picturise it growing up. It's very complex. There are extreme highs and equal lows, from time to time. Sometimes you feel very confused and sometimes everything makes perfect sense."

"Ooohoo... philosopher, I need to keep the phone down. My bill is shooting. You can also call me sometimes, you miser. I will wait for your call. Chalo...bye bye.", Varsha hung up the phone.

Mridula wanted to talk more. She wanted to open her heart out to her as she used to before marriage. She longed to take an unbiased opinion about whatever was going on in her life. She couldn't tell those things to her mother, as she didn't know how she would respond. She obviously couldn't open up with her Bhabhi as it would have then definitely reached her brother's ears and eventually her parents.

***

Mridula was blessed with a baby girl. They named her Chavi. Most of the times now Mridula was busy with her baby. She loved to give Chavi an oil massage and a bath thereafter. She was learning to do and finish her work faster and she tried to juggle her time between house chores, her daughter and her own healthcare and upkeep. She was learning that if she didn't take care of herself, she couldn't take care of her daughter and others in the house. Apoorva kept busy with his work on the weekdays. On the weekends, either he was sleeping or liked to go out for a movie and dinner, in short, he just wanted to relax. If she asked him, on the days when he had an off from office, to change Chavi's diaper or to look after her for some time, while she rested or ran some errands, he simply refused. He felt that it was not his job to take care of the child. He thought that she should have managed her time to take care of Chavi. He didn't like to be disturbed during the nights as well, when Chavi woke up crying, on the other hand he asked Mridula to take her to the other room to pacify her. Mridula was mostly tired those days because Chavi hardly slept at night and took short naps throughout the day. Mridula's mom told her to rest while the baby rested during the daytime, but it was usually not possible for her as she had to bathe, eat, and do the household work at that time.

Time flew by, soon enough Chavi started crawling.

One morning Apoorva was getting ready for the office. Mridula was in the kitchen, preparing breakfast. Just outside the kitchen, Chavi was in her crib playing with a toy tied to the handle of her crib. Mridula was checking on her in between her cooking. Seema and Rajendra were in their room.

Apoorva came to the kitchen in a huff, "I asked you to take out my clothes. Where are they?"

Mridula looked up from kadhai, "Got busy, so I couldn't. Why don't you take them yourself."

"If I have to take them myself then couldn't you open your bloody mouth and say that in the first place?"

"I wanted to do it, then was caught up with Chavi. What's the big deal. Instead of wasting your time coming here to complain about it, couldn't you take them out yourself."

"Big deal? You ask me big deal? You got busy; you could have asked Ravi to do it. Basically, I can't rely on you for the smallest of things."

"You yourself could tell him that, couldn't you."

"Tell me you are good for nothing; I will do everything myself. I am fully capable of that. I don't need you."

"What! Are you perfect with everything yourself? If that's what you think then you can take care of your things yourself, I guess."

Apoorva raised his right hand, "Shut up you woman or you will get a tight slap. I am already getting late and she's going on arguing here. Rascal!"

Rajendra Verma came out of his room, "Why, you two have started in the morning! Stop it! See you have scared the child." He pointed at Chavi, who had started howling by that time, "Mridula, what kind of a mother are you? Don't you see how your child is distressed by your shouting?"

Apoorva stomped out of the house.

Seema also came and stood in the doorway of their room, "Now, he is going out empty stomach. What is the need to make a ruckus over something as small as 'handing over clothes?"

Mridula stood there dumbfounded. She was surprised that her in-laws were unconcerned, unruffled by the misbehaviour of their son. It was an acceptable behaviour for a man to be angry over a trivial matter and misbehave with his wife. On the other hand, the wife should mind her behaviour and should not retaliate.

It was a striking contrast to her own upbringing, where respect was paramount. She had expected a supportive response from her in -laws, perhaps a gesture of remorse over their son's behaviour. Instead, their indifference left her feeling isolated, as if she was the only one who saw the problem. This lack of concern not only baffled her but also made her question the values they held as a family.

In the evening, when Apoorva came back from office, he behaved as if nothing had happened. When Mridula mentioned to him about his rude behaviour in the morning. He apologised for the same and asked her to forget it. He said that she too lost her cool in the fight, so, it was even. She also thought that he must have been tense, as he was getting late, so he must have misbehaved unintentionally. She thought of pardoning him and moving on, after all he loved her so much.

***

Few days later

It was a Sunday morning. Rajendra was expecting someone from a bank. He had to get some fixed deposits done in the name of Seema and himself. He wasn't feeling very well to visit the branch, so he requested a bank official to help him with it, at home. Ravi had taken Chavi outside in the garden, in a stroller, for some fresh air.

Rajendra and Apoorva, after having finished their breakfast, were sitting on a sofa in the drawing room. Mridula was taking her breakfast at the dining table.

The bank assistant entered the drawing room, "Namaste sir, I am Vipin from ICICI."

Rajendra and Vipin got engaged in conversation and some paperwork. Apoorva was overlooking them from his newspaper. He looked at Mridula, who was taking out something from the refrigerator, kept in the corner, near the dining table. He kept looking at her, who then moved into the kitchen without noticing Apoorva.

Apoorva followed her into the kitchen, "Aren't you supposed to offer tea or drinks to the visitors? Offer them water, at least."

"Yeah! Was about to."

"When? After he leaves?"

"I had my hands full; I will ask just now."

"Don't try to bullshit me. You have not been taught simple manners to ask guests for tea/coffee."

"Why don't you go and ask him, what would he like to have? I will make it."

"That's not my job. Go and do it yourself."

Mridula went in the drawing room and asked him as to what he would like to have. She served them and went upstairs in their room.

After Vipin left, Apoorva went straight to their room. He started shouting at her, "Do you need an invitation for yourself, to ask visitors for water and drinks? Isn't it a basic courtesy you should follow?"

"I told you; I was about to. If I had not, couldn't you ask him instead?", somewhere she felt that Apoorva himself could also ask if she didn't. He was just browsing the newspaper after all. She, on the other hand, was in the middle of her breakfast. What was the big deal in Apoorva asking him that? He too could serve him water.

Before she could properly explain herself that why she didn't, Apoorva lost his temper, "Couldn't you ask first and do whatever you were doing later? You always play defensive instead of accepting your mistake. Accept your mistake and say that you did it on purpose."

"I was busy, you could also do it, simple. Don't eat my head by harping on the same thing."

"You bloody well accept your mistake, you bitch! Just deflecting like a weakling."

"How dare you? You are weak not me."

Apoorva raised his hand and barged towards her, "You will argue with me? I will give you a tight one, your face will fall off. You, you...."

"Go on, go on, hit me!"

Apoorva grinded his teeth in anger, lowered his hand and pushed her forcefully on to the bed instead. She went off balance. In order to break the fall, she waved her hands in the air, and she landed on her left hand, which twisted by the force of her fall. She screamed in pain. Apoorva wanted to hit her but went out of the room instead.

Mridula started sobbing. Apoorva came back after some time to apologise. He said he felt very bad about his behaviour. He couldn't control his anger when she tried to blame him instead of accepting her mistake. He didn't mean to hurt her. He promised never to repeat such a behaviour again. He hugged her and kissed her.

Mridula didn't say a thing and quietly went away from there. She set out thinking that such episodes were becoming quite a regular feature. Initially she thought that he was probably worked up or had just had a bad day which was why he was edgy. But no, even when he was sitting leisurely it could happen. She was unable to predict his behaviour. He had been so loving and caring at moments that she could not believe that it was the same guy who was so ruthless and insolent. On her birthday, he had taken half a day off. He had brought her favourite sweet. They went shopping for her. He encouraged her to buy whatever she liked even the slightest bit. They dined at Hyatt Regency where he had planned a small surprise for her.

Why would he not show any patience with her, to listen to her point of view when it came to small things, which were so insignificant to throw a fuss about. She wanted to ask and discuss with someone. She tried talking to him when he was in a good mood. His reply was that he expected her to listen to him and yes, he was temperamental since childhood. She tried talking to Seema, but she was evasive and said the same thing that he was like that only. She tried to drop hints to her mother about his bad temper and language, who straight away told her to come back and leave such a guy. Her mother even asked her whether she should discuss it with her father? Mridula didn't want to bother her father, so she discouraged her mother from it. Then she stopped telling her.

She knew that Apoorva loved her. But it felt hypocritical to her that he demanded her absolute compliance while ignoring her opinions and feelings. She struggled to understand how he could justify his actions, acting as if his desires were the only ones that mattered. This double standard left her feeling frustrated and undervalued, as if her voice didn't count in their relationship. Shouldn't mutual respect be the foundation of their partnership? It became increasingly clear that they needed to address this imbalance if they were ever to find common ground. She was not his subordinate.

One day, while she was five months pregnant and felt very sick, she didn't feel like going out and wanted him to be with her, but he went to watch a movie with his friends instead, stating that he got very few holidays and couldn't spend them sitting at home. Very recently, when she was running hundred and two fever, still, he and his parents had gone out to have chole bhature, leaving her and a few months old Chavi at home because Seema had a craving to have them. They had asked Ravi to make khichdi for her. Whereas whenever Apoorva was ill or needed her, she was always there to took care of him. Mridula was mulling over it and was feeling extremely low.

Was she being treated like that because she wasn't earning, or was it because she was a woman? She was utterly confused. Whenever she discussed it with him, he would always have an explanation like, "mom was really wanting to go.... or you can do whatever you like...., no one stops you.... don't cook up things in your head.... it is all feminism shit, and I don't think like that."

CHAPTER SEVEN

Summer of 2006

It was Chavi's birthday that day. She had turned one. Rajendra had got the whole house decorated with colourful balloons and streamers. It was one of those rare days when Seema was helping Mridula in the kitchen to turn out delicious delicacies. Apoorva had to come in early with the customised cake in 'Minnie mouse' shape.

Chavi had developed diarrhoea at the last moment. Mridula had given her medication after consulting the doctor over phone. They all were waiting for Apoorva as guests had started pouring in. They had called Rajendra's friends, Seema's friends, their immediate neighbours and Apoorva's friends.

Apoorva entered an hour later with a huge cake box. Placed it on the dining table, greeted everyone and excused himself to go to the washroom. Ravi opened the cake box to take out the cake. Seema supervised him to lay it in a big glass plate and placed the candles on it. Chavi toddled to Mridula and started tugging at her saree. Mridula took her in her arms and realised that she needed a diaper change. She took her to her in-law's bedroom and started changing her. Her attention was diverted to the other side of the bed, where Apoorva's wallet, car keys and phone were lying. His phone was flashing and vibrating every few seconds and some messages were coming.

After finishing with Chavi and leaving her in the drawing room with Rajendra, she went back to the room. She picked up his phone and started to read the messages. They were from some Shefali Malhotra, "Have you reached home? Was the wifey red with anger? How did everyone like the cake? Will be calling you at the usual time...."

Before Mridula could go through rest of the messages of previous days, she heard the flush and water running in the washroom. She placed the phone on the bed and went to the kitchen. She was furious but she had to contain herself till everyone left.

Later that night, Mridula and Apoorva were in their room. She had put Chavi to sleep in her cot, kept adjacent to her bed. Inside her head, she was preparing herself for what and how she would ask him about the messages.

"Who is Shefali?"

"Hmmm...uhh, why? She is a client. Why? How do you know her?"

"Is she a friend too?"

"What do you mean? Told you she is a client. What are you trying to say?"

"I meant, are you close to her? Do you discuss personal things and all."

"What do you exactly want to know?"

"Apoorva, I saw her messages on your phone. Drop that acting."

"You were checking my phone? When? Why do you need to check my phone?"

"Need I didn't have. It was buzzing and flashing repeatedly, I happened to read some messages."

"And... what did you read?"

"Leave aside what I read. Your answer is what I want. Is she your close friend? A confidant?"

"Close friend? No! But yes, we have to be friendly with the clients in order to gain their confidence. To know them better."

"Do you need to share with them each and every detail of your day? Who do you think I am, a fool?"

Apoorva burst out laughing and took her in his embrace, "Arree baba, who is calling you a fool. You are very smart. But here, you are unnecessarily taxing yourself. She had come to the office today, so I shared with her that it's Chavi's birthday. I told her that I needed to leave early for home and pick up the cake on the way. That's all."

"Why was she messaging to enquire everything?"

"Nothing like that. It was just a courtesy inquiry. We had such a lovely day. Chavi was so happy. Don't spoil it by thinking rubbish. Is this a new nighty you are wearing?"

"No, it's old. Do not change the topic. Deflection is a sign of weak defence."

"Ooh! Where did you learn that? Impressive!" He started tickling and teasing her.

"Stop it, Apoorva! Ok, you asked for it. Here I come!"

She too started tickling him. They both ended up in each other's arms. Apoorva kissed her passionately and his hands slipped down to undo her buttons. She curled her legs around him in anticipation and longing.

***

Six months later

Six months had passed since Chavi's first birthday. She had started babbling and running. She was quite a handful for adults around her. The minute Mridula took her attention away from her, she would do something mischievous. She was growing up at a lightning speed. Mridula had not been keeping too well lately. She was always tired and caught cold and cough very easily and frequently.

Apoorva had come home from work. Seema instructed Ravi, "Go get water for bhaiya. Also put water on gas for four cups of tea."

Apoorva spoke while handing over some papers to Mridula, "I collected some of your reports from the lab on my way back. Rest of the reports will come tomorrow. I have asked them to send it on my e-mail. Can't go to their office again and again and waste my time."

"I can pick-up from their office tomorrow."

"No need. You need not bother to go all the way there. You are unwell and will unnecessarily tire yourself. They will send it. I have given my e-mail address since I couldn't remember yours. We can email them to Dr. Chaddha. Then let him tell what further course of action needs to be taken."

Next evening, Seema and Rajendra were having tea in the garden. Rajendra had been advised rest and strict diet monitoring. His blood pressure and sugar, both were burgeoning out of control. Seema was most of the times with him to supervise his routine.

Apoorva was upstairs in his study printing some documents on the printer attached to the desktop. He was preparing papers for a case, which were needed the next day. He had asked Mridula not to disturb him for a couple of hours.

Mridula was feeding a banana to Chavi in the dining room. She was also supervising Ravi who was doing dinner preparations in the kitchen.

Mridula's phone rang and she picked it up, "Hello, yes. Ok...hunh...yes, thank you so much."

She finished feeding Chavi, asked Ravi to keep an eye on her and went upstairs. She had received a call from the laboratory saying that they had mailed her the reports. She wanted to extract them from the desktop.

She asked Apoorva, who was busy with printing, "Listen, my reports have come. We can extract them and mail them to the doctor now."

"You may do it later once I am finished. Or I will do it if I find time."

She went downstairs and waited for him to finish his work. By the time he came down it was almost dinner time.

"Have you taken out my reports?"

"I forgot. I will do it after dinner."

Mridula's disappointment showed on her face.

"You can go and do it yourself in case you are in a hurry."

After serving dinner to everyone, Mridula went upstairs to take out the reports. When she opened his mail, she realised that she didn't have his password. She called on his mobile from the study to ask him, instead of going downstairs.

"Leave it, I will do it later."

"No, give me the password I want to finish it."

"What is the hurry?"

"You don't want to give me, right?"

"Take it yaar! I don't have anything to hide. It's Apu12......"

After she finished mailing the reports to the doctor, her mind started pacing..., "Was Appu trying to hide something from me, that is why he didn't want to give his mail password? Should I go through his mails? "

She wanted to be sure but at the same time feared that her doubt might turn out to be true.

She opened his email again. She started browsing through the 'Inbox'. Nothing seemed to be suspicious, just regular correspondence. Maybe he had deleted his emails.

She browsed through the sent mails, spam and junk mails too. Nothing. She took a sigh of relief.

As she was closing the window, it struck her to check the messenger once. She again opened his mail. There, in the messenger, she spotted 'Shefali Malhotra.' She froze for a few seconds, came back to her senses and opened the chat. The chat poured on to the screen. She started reading....

It was a couple of hours to midnight. Mridula had already put Chavi to sleep.

"I want to talk."

Apoorva's whole attention was on his phone screen, "shoot!"

"I need you to be attentive. Leave your phone."

Apoorva kept his phone on the side table, "I am listening, tell me."

"What is going on between you and Shefali?"

"Told you already. She is a client. Why are you bothering me again and again for this?"

"I don't feel it is limited to that."

"You are over thinking. Don't waste your time and energy on useless things and utilise it in something worthwhile."

"Apoorva, either you will divulge what is brewing or I......."

"You what? When there is nothing why are you wasting our time?"

Mridula raised her voice, "Listen, if you are not confessing, I can give you proof."

"Proof? What proof?"

"Ok, I have read your conversations."

"So, I converse with her for her case. And by the way where have you read our conversations? Do you snoop into my phone?"

"So, you will not give up this facade that easily? Hmmm... I read your yahoo messenger messages."

"Who does that? Why on earth will you do such a thing?"

"That is not the point here. The point is what is going on? You are having an affair? You are two timing?"

"What makes you think that? Yes, she has become a friend. So what? That doesn't mean I am having an affair."

"You crib to her about how dissatisfied you are in life. She addresses you as 'dear'. You call her 'sweets'. You tell her smallest of things that's happening in your life. What else is an affair?", She was now at the top of her voice.

Chavi woke up from all the clamour, sat up and started crying. Mridula took her in her arms and pacified her, rocking from side to side. She went back to sleep.

Apoorva started, "Agreed, she might be a little more than a client. What's the big deal? She's become a good friend. Don't I need a let out. She understands me and I understand her."

"Wow! A friend! Who am I to you then? Wasn't it you who told me that a girl and a boy can never be just friends. There is bound to be some attraction somewhere, always.", she snorted.

Apoorva realised that he was cornered, and he couldn't escape this one, "Yes, it might not be all platonic, it's not physical either. She is a beautiful attractive woman but that doesn't mean that I am sleeping around with her."

She couldn't believe her ears; how shamelessly callous he was. He was admitting to being attracted to another woman. Would he be able to take it if she praised any other man in front of him? It was disconcerting to hear him talk about her like that.

"Why do I believe you? How do I believe you? You might be lying."

"I don't desire anyone other than you Mridu.", he came closer and tried to hug her.

She gently pushed him away, "No! No need. You are so...how could you......". She wanted to say a lot but stopped mid-way. There was no point. She was deeply hurt. "Let's sleep. You have to go to work, and I too have to get up early."

Sleep was far away from her eyes. She kept twisting and turning in bed till dawn. Then she must have dosed off for a couple of hours in the early morning.

CHAPTER EIGHT

Summer of 2007

It had been a few months since the day Mridula and Apoorva had a heart to heart regarding Shefali. Since then, they both had mostly kept to themselves and only talked when mundane routine required them to do so. Apoorva had shown no sign of remorse on what he had been doing. In fact, now that she was observing him more closely, she found him possessing a flirtatious nature. He on the other hand, kind of gloated about how women still found him attractive, even after three years of marriage.

Mridula tried to give a hint regarding Apoorva's behaviour to her mother-in-law but pretty soon she realised that a mother would never feel that her son could be in the wrong and would seldom agree with her daughter in law's perspective, especially when they were not in congruence with her son's views. In her eyes, her son would always be an innocent creature, who is struggling with life's endless, unfair ordeals. Mridula never felt that connect with her father-in-law ever, to confide in him anyway.

Mridula's brother had moved to an independent house, away from his parents, two years ago. Her mother and father were feeling very lonely after he had gone, although he came to visit them, a couple of times every month, along with his family. He had been blessed with a daughter, who now was a year old.

Mridula desperately wanted some time away from Apoorva and his parents, to assess him, his behaviour; determine the course of action she should take and consider the future of their relationship. She had to contemplate as to what she wanted from life, from their marriage. She made up her mind to talk to him in the evening, after he returned from the Chambers.

After dinner, Apoorva and Mridula had gone to their room. Apoorva was looking at Chavi playing, who was trying to put colourful rings on a stand. She clapped after every successful attempt and looked towards her parents for appreciation.

Mridula took a deep breath and started, "Can I take your time and attention?"

"Hmmm. I am listening."

"I am confused."

"For what?"

"Everything. I don't know what I want from life? I don't know what gives me happiness? Whether I am happy for the way things are going on between us?"

"If you don't know then who else would?"

"Do you know what you want from life?"

Apoorva looked at Mridula and sighed, "Huh!" Then looked away. It Looked like he was contemplating. After a couple of minutes, he spoke, "I know for sure what makes me happy. What I want. I want to be happy and comfortable in life. I want my family to be comfortable as well."

"Can you be unhappy and keep others happy at the same time? That is the question. What comes first for you, you or your family?"

"If one is unhappy, how can one keep others happy?". Apoorva looked into her eyes, questioning, "What kind of a question is that? Are you not happy?"

"Sort of."

"Either you are, or you are not. What is this 'sort of'?"

"Let me put it this way, I am dissatisfied with a lot of things. Since I am not convinced with many things, it makes me sad. Sad because neither can I accept them nor change them."

"Why don't you say clearly what's bothering you, instead of playing riddles."

"I will try. See, I have chosen you. With you comes your family. If I don't like certain things in you or your family, should I leave you? But I don't want to do that because I feel attached to you. Leaving everything is also not a solution in my understanding. But then...."

"You are saying that you would like to leave me. Is that right?"

"No, no... I am saying I am confused.", she was scared at the thought of leaving the family she had created and nurtured so dearly.

"What do you want Mridu? I promise, I will do whatever you say and whatever makes you happy."

"That is exactly what I don't know."

"Ok, you take your time. Think about it. I will also contemplate. Then we can talk and work out something. Fine?"

"Hmmm."

***

A Few days later

It was a pleasant evening after a heavy downpour. The temperature had dropped several notches, bringing relief from the scorching heat of Delhi. Apoorva had come back from chambers earlier than his usual time, as Mridula had asked him to. They had decided to go out for dinner, just the two of them.

They had asked Ravi and Seema to take care of Chavi during the time they would have been out. Seema had agreed reluctantly, she could not refuse her son.

Mridula came down the staircase, she wore a red and a peacock blue suit. She had put on some lipstick as well after.... she couldn't remember when was the last time she had applied it. Her hair was tied in a high bun over her head. Apoorva looked at her and kept looking, till she stepped on to the ground floor and stood near him.

"I am ready to go.", said Mridula

They had chosen a restaurant which was usually less crowded. Their service was also very relaxed. They settled down and ordered food. Apoorva was humming while casually looking around. Mridula cleared her throat to speak.

"You had asked me to think about what I want?"

"Yes of course! Have you come up with any ideas?" Apoorva extended his left hand on the table, intending her to place hers over it. She hesitated for a moment then placed her right hand over it.

"Did you think about it? You said you would.", she enquired.

"I did some evaluation of my own. I think you are stressed after having a baby. You are unable to handle the burden of baby's responsibility along with the household duties."

Mridula looked at him surprised. Either he didn't understand, or he didn't care. Either way there was no purpose in trying to explain to him that she felt lost, lost about her place in his life, lost about her own deep desires, which had disappeared in fulfilling her duties as a wife, as a daughter-in-law and now as a mother. Somewhere down the line she had lost touch with her own self. She was unclear whether her ego was hurt, or her self-respect was at stake. She pulled her hand back from his grip.

"I have given it a serious contemplation. And after some thoughtful and sincere consideration, I have come to a conclusion."

"Alright. What is your conclusion?"

"We have come a long way from where we started. We are not the same as we were when we got married. We have forgotten the very purpose for which we wanted to be with each other. We are very different from what we perceived each other to be.", she paused.

He was now looking straight into her eyes, "And... what is the solution for this conclusion according to you?"

"We need to take a step back, reflect, introspect, fathom what exactly we want out of life. Then we start afresh."

"Sounds great. But how do we do that?"

"We take a break in our relationship.", she said plainly. She had been preparing herself to say this for the past few days.

"What? If you are saying what I think you are, then what about Chavi?"

"She should be with me since no one else can look after her as I can."

"I feel it is not fair to separate her from her father." He took a pause, then spoke again, "I know where you are coming from. I am not asking you to exonerate me or anything, but no one does like this either, for such petty issues...such....", he stuttered. He was so sure that she could never leave him; he was not prepared for this at all.

"I don't know about others, neither do I care."

Ground was shaking under him. He couldn't believe his ears. But his ego got the better of him quickly, "If you want a break then so be it. Tell me how long a break do you want? Or do you want a permanent break? I am fine with that too."

"Don't go the ego way. I am talking about a break not a divorce."

"Why not? It is as good as that only. You want freedom, have full freedom. Why have only half."

He hung his head and closed his eyes to think. After a few minutes he spoke, "How long do you want this break?"

"I don't know. I can't say."

"Then let us make it mutual. We will start all over again, once you are ok and I am ready to be with you again. We both should be comfortable and agree to start all over again. Alright?"

"I am good with this arrangement."

"Good. Let me know when you would like to go, I will book your tickets.

CHAPTER NINE

Early 2008

Indore

Morning time was always a rush time for Mridula. It had been six months since she had come from Delhi with Chavi. She had taken up her old job again within a few days of coming back to Indore. Her boss was too happy to have her back. Her mother Rama was also very pleased to have Mridula and Chavi's company, as she felt lonely after both her kids had flown out of the nest. Rama took care of Chavi in Mridula's absence. Sudeep, Mridula's father, was very upset to hear about her decision and didn't approve of their arrangement of taking a break in their relationship. According to him 'out of sight, out of mind' always proved to be true in life. But, at the same time, he couldn't close his doors on his daughter. With time even he had accepted their presence, in fact, he loved spending time with young Chavi and in no time became used to them being around.

It's in man's nature to quickly adapt to the new environment and circumstances. Mridula too had that ability. She had now adjusted to her new routine and life in Indore. She readied Chavi in the mornings for her play school, dropped her off till the cycle rickshaw. The cycle rickshaw took her to the school and brought her back home around noon, where Rama would wait for her outside the house, as the rickshaw dropped her off. After dropping her in the morning, Mridula got ready for her office and came back in the evenings. After that she spent time with Chavi and helped her mother in the kitchen for dinner. She talked to Apoorva when he called to speak with his daughter or when she called him after Chavi pestered her to speak to her father. Sometimes she thought about what would become of her future, but then she quickly diverted her thoughts to mundane work and tried not to worry too much or dwell into it for long.

When Gaurav came to know about his sister's struggle and upheaval in life, he told her that she was a real-life hero. She might not be possessing any superpowers like fictional superheroes, but she had the mental strength of one. She was dealing with her problems with utmost mental toughness and maturity which made him proud of her as a brother.

It being a Sunday, Gaurav, Naina and their daughter, Jaanvi, were coming for lunch. Chavi and Jaanvi had become friends. They were almost the same age. They were double mischievous when they were together and brought the whole house down. "They definitely work as balm for sore eyes", said their granddad, Sudeep.

Rama and Mridula were busy in the kitchen preparing delectable delicacies. Rama possessed the knack of preparing the most delicious dishes, effortlessly. Naina too joined them in the kitchen, after she came.

Gaurav and Sudeep went to Sudeep's room to discuss about how his business was doing and to do some other manly talks, after they all had finished lunch. Rama took Chavi and Jaanvi and retired to her room to have a siesta. Naina and Mridula were resting on Mridula's bed and chatting.

Naina rolled over to pop her head on her hand, "I am happy that you chose to be proactive rather than reactive in your life, Mridu? By the way how is work?"

"Work is demanding but I am enjoying."

"Does Chavi miss her dad?"

"She talks to him when she likes. We both are coping well."

They both continued to share and pour their hearts out to each other.

"It's not fair to compare our lives but if I do, just for the sake of comparing, Gaurav always understood my point of view, in any given situation. Whereas in your case, Apoorva doesn't seem to possess such a sensibility or sensitivity. I feel that you have taken the right step or let's say taken a step back. Your work will be a let out for your creativity. I think you have totally lost touch with that side of yourself.", she smiled at Mridula and continued, "On an unrelated note, I met your class fellow, at a restaurant in Vijay Nagar. He recognised me and came to say 'hello'. At first, I was confused and didn't recognise him, but then recalled seeing him with you, outside the house, when you returned from college."

Mridula was startled, "Who? Sumit?", she said wide eyed.

"Uhh,...the one you told lived in the lane adjacent to ours."

"But he went to the US. Has he come back?", Mridula asked, her voice ringing with curiosity.

"He must have. He told me that he has opened a dance academy or something in Vijay Nagar. I had gone there with Gaurav to see a property. I was waiting at a table in a restaurant, for Gaurav, to bring us something to eat, when he came up to me. He was asking your whereabouts. I told him that you are back in Indore now for some time. Before we could exchange numbers, he left in a huff. I think he saw Gaurav returning to the seat."

"Oh! ok. Vijay Nagar is the suburbs, right?"

"Yeah! The area has really grown in the last few years."

Naina dosed off after a heavy meal. But Mridula was awake. Memories of Sumit came flooding back to her. She remembered how they had met. He was a new student in the class. He wanted notebooks to complete his work. He had come to her for science notebook. He had very hesitantly asked her for the notebook. Then she recalled, how they slowly became friends and eventually grew fond of each other. They were always spotted together thereafter. She remembered the Tincha Fall, Sumit's proposal and his pining for her. She stirred in bed, recollected how she avoided him after Apoorva came into her life. How rejected and dejected he must have felt, she felt bad for him. She couldn't help but think that how her life would have been if she had chosen Sumit over Apoorva. She always thought that Apoorva was more mature than Sumit, was more sorted and stable. In hindsight, she doubted her conviction, her decision. She felt a strong sense of empathy towards Sumit.

***

Summer of 2008

Indore

"The traffic is more than the usual today.", she thought. Maybe she felt it more because she was eager to reach her destination.

Mridula had been searching for the dance academies in Indore, on the internet, whenever she got a chance to be alone in her office. Internet had been recently installed by her boss. She had some probable numbers after several attempts. Out of a few phone numbers, she had noted down, she started dialling them up, one by one, to confirm, which one was Sumit's. She could not speak a word for some time, when she heard his voice, on the other side. Only when she recovered from her numbness, after a moments pause, could she speak. Her hands were sweaty, and her voice broke, "Hi! Guess who?", she mustered strength and spoke.

They decided to meet the next day, in the evening, at a small restaurant. She had left her office, two hours earlier than the usual time. He was coming straight from the academy after his class, where he taught western dance forms to students. She didn't want to take a chance of going to his house, lest any acquaintance would see her there. For the same reason, he had not gone to hers. Somewhere he was hesitant about meeting her, after all, she had been avoiding him after she had met Apoorva.

She opened the glass door of the entrance to the restaurant, stepped inside, her eyes scanned the rows of people dining there. To her left, in the far end of the room, she spotted him, waving at her. She went in his direction.

"Look at you, you look just the same after six years.", Sumit grinning from cheek to cheek.

"And you look younger than before.", Mridula beaming.

"I guess it's my dance routine."

Both laughed.

"How have you been? Tell me from the start....", Sumit said looking into her eyes.

The time just flew by when they were together. Mridula checked her watch, realised that it was already late for her to reach home, she sprung up from her chair.

"What's the hurry? When will you meet me again?"

"Soon, pretty soon."

After that day, they met each other whenever they could squeeze out some time. They met on lunch, they went for shopping, sometimes they even watched a movie. Sumit was not married or seeing anyone. He stayed alone. She also went to his residence a couple of times.

***

A month later

Mridula was sitting on a couch of Sumit's one bedroom flat. He was in the kitchen preparing tea for both of them.

"I am glad that you came back to India.", Mridula said slightly raising her voice so that it could reach him in the kitchen.

"As I told you, I was very home sick.", replied Sumit. He got two cups of tea and a plate of biscuits in a tray and sat down next to her. "I saw good prospects of a dance academy in Indore, as compared to Bangalore." His parents had moved back to Bangalore after he had gone to the US.

"We were destined to meet. That is why you came here."

"If I tell you that somewhere I was hoping to see you again, will you believe me?"

Mridula didn't say anything but instead, nodded her head softly. They sat in silence for some time.

Mridula spoke and broke the silence, "I want to apologise to you. Don't ask me 'why'. I think you know."

It was his turn to nod now. He kept his cup down and held her hand. She too kept down hers. She felt her cheeks flushing and a drop of sweat trickling down her back. She was nervous and excited at the same time. She waited for him to make the first move. He moved closer to her and took her in his arms. She didn't resist rather hugged him back. Feeling encouraged he took her face in his hands and placed his lips on to hers, slowly sucking her lower lip.

Mridula gently pushed him away from her, "I better be going." She knew if she stayed back, she would not be able to refuse him. She didn't want that.

"Chavi must be waiting for me."

"Mridu please.... please stay!"

"Don't stop me. I am afraid I can't, although every cell in my body wants to. I guess certain things are just not meant to be."

Sumit was quite upset but told her, "I will be the last person to pressurise you for anything. But I want to say that just for once, don't let your brain lead your heart. Have faith in the higher power and take a blind leap. Nothing is random in the world. Behind every existence and every happening, there operates an invisible hand working for a larger purpose, which we may not recognise at that time, but it perfectly fits like any thread in the tapestry of life."

"I guess I need more time."

"Time for what?"

"To contemplate."

After the episode, Mridula avoided to go to Sumit's place. She insisted to meet at public places only.

CHAPTER TEN

Autumn of 2008

Indore

It was a usual day at work. Mridula was discussing some textile patterns with her colleague. She gave instructions to the office staff and opened her laptop to write an e-mail; just then her phone rang. It was Apoorva. She cut the call and resumed her work. She didn't want to take his call while working. It rang again. This time she picked up, thinking it must me something important enough for him to call again.

"Hello....I am at work. "

"Hellooo....", said Apoorva in a shaky voice.

"What is it", she asked, gauging something was wrong.

"Mridu......papa... he left us."

"What? But we talked on Sunday. He was alright then. How come....", her voice trailed off.

"It was massive cardiac arrest. I thought that I should inform....", he said clearing his voice.

"Of course! You did the right thing. I am in shock. I don't know what to say. Really a sad news. You take care of yourself and mummy."

"Hmmm.... ok. I will go now, some arrangements to be done." He disconnected the call.

Later at home, Mridula gave the news to everyone. Sudeep insisted that she should go to Delhi. He arranged for a flight ticket for her for the next morning. She packed her bags and kept some extra clothes and toys, just in case she had to stay back for a longer period, informed her office and went to sleep.

***

Early 2009

New Delhi

It had been six months since Mridula and Chavi had come from Indore. Apoorva had apologised for his behaviour and convinced Mridula to not to return to Indore. He had promised her that he would stay away from Shefali and would be more patient with her. He had also assured her to give her space and that he would not misbehave with her. She decided to forgive him yet once again and thought of giving him another chance. She had informed her parents about her decision to stay back in Delhi. She had then gone to Indore after a few days, to get her remaining belongings and inform her office.

There she went to meet Sumit too. She felt it was imperative to do that since last time too she had not bid him proper farewell. He couldn't say much to her. He looked far away pensively and commented, "Unlike nature's laws, the beauty of man-made laws is that they are not uniform in nature. They come in different measures for different people, and they are smartly woven around the loopholes. I hope you stay happy in your life. As for me, you are my first love and will always remain that."

She left him with a heavy heart and cried all the way home. She felt weak in the stomach as if someone had punched her to leave a dull pain there.

After she came back to Delhi, she enrolled Chavi in a play school. Slowly they settled in their new routine.

One day when Mridula was resting in her room, in the afternoon, after a hectic day, her mobile phone rang.

"Hello mamma, how are you?"

"Don't ask me that. How will I be in an empty house? You have forgotten your mother completely."

"How is it possible? How can I forget you? Today morning itself Chavi was asking about you. I told her that we will talk to Nani and Nana in the evening. I would have called you after teatime if you wouldn't have."

"I miss you and Chavi so much. Gaurav and Jaanvi also do not come that often now. Your Papa is always busy in watching news on TV or reading it in a newspaper. He doesn't step out of the house after his last illness. He always complains of being tired."

"Ma, I miss you too but what to do, this is life. You must convince papa to go out for walks at least. Slowly he will recover from the weakness."

"I do tell him that, but I guess he exhausts himself out fast now. I feel he doesn't have any motivation to push himself. I talk to you and unburden myself, but he misses Gaurav a lot, as he doesn't have that closeness with anyone else. He doesn't have anyone else to talk to." Rama started sobbing. "I am very happy that you have gone back to your house and are happy there. But I feel very alone now."

Mridula consoled her. She cheered her up by telling her that she would try to visit her as soon as possible.

"I can come for a week's time. I will book the ticket today. Don't get disheartened like this."

"That will be so good. Still, it's not a permanent solution for our desolation. You will have to go back to your house."

Mridula was gloomy when she came down with Chavi in the evening. She made tea for herself and Seema and hot chocolate for Chavi.

After her father-in-law's death, Mridula had begun to open up to Seema more than before. Mridula felt that she needed her support after Rajendra's passing away. She made efforts in taking care of her and making small talks every now and then. Slowly she saw the change in Seema too. She no longer was as critical of her as she used to be.

She took the tea tray in her room and served her.

"What's the matter?", Asked Seema looking at her face.

"Nothing, why?"

"Your eyes look despondent."

"Do they? Hmmm. Actually, mummy had called. She ......", she told her about Rama's call. While she was narrating it, Apoorva entered the room. He had just returned from the Chambers. He too heard her and learned about her parent's loneliness. He asked Ravi to get him coffee and sat down on a chair kept in the corner of the room.

"Your parents feel unhappy because of loneliness which is quite understandable at their age. Mummy speaks out but papa keeps it in his heart. I feel I should talk to Gaurav about shifting back to the house to stay with them. What do you think? I know that he will regret later, for sure, if he doesn't act now." Apoorva had always felt close to Mridula's parents. Similarly, her parents had always liked him. Even after they both had taken break in their relationship, that mutual respect remained.

"I have already mentioned this to bhaiya. He has some apprehensions regarding mom's behaviour towards Naina. But I know that mom has changed, she too has evolved, learned from life. She now knows that if she is not accommodative or understanding towards Naina, she would be left alone in life."

"I can talk to him if you want. I think he trusts me." Gaurav had unsaid faith in Apoorva since the day he had saved him from the goons in his office.

"You can give it a try; I see no harm in that."

Apoorva called up Gaurav and convinced him to move back with his parents. He helped him understand that they could all support each other if they stayed together, and it would be healthier for Jaanvi to grow up with her grandparents. Expenses are also less per head in a joint family, compared to nuclear ones. Expense point helped the most in making up his mind to move back. He respected Apoorva's thought that he might regret later after his parents were gone, if he didn't move in with them while there was still time.

The day Gaurav moved back; Mridula was very happy. She thanked Apoorva and they all went out for dinner to celebrate it.

They were sitting in an Italian restaurant in south Delhi. It was jam packed since it was a weekend. Their order finally arrived after waiting for more than half an hour.

Mridula gave a slice of pizza to Chavi, "It's yummy, hmmmm.... try it. Liked it?"

"Yeah! What is Dadi eating? I want that too." Chavi was almost four now and spoke full sentences. She was developing her likes and dislikes. She wanted to eat and dress as per her own will.

"Here try it, give me your plate, I will give you some.", Seema gave some Ravioli to Chavi out of her plate. While she was serving her, she gave a double glance towards her right. This did not go unnoticed with Mridula. Throughout the dinner she felt that Seema was slightly uncomfortable after that. She kept looking in the same direction from the corner of her eye. Seema also adjusted her kurta and hair a couple of times. Mridula looked in the direction where Seema was looking and noticed an elderly man looking towards them. When she looked at him, he became conscious and looked away. She was completely puzzled and curious at the same time about what was going on.

Once they came back home, Mridula quickly changed and came down to Seema's room.

She knocked and entered. Seema was in the washroom. She sat down in a chair and waited for her. Seema opened the door of the washroom and was startled to see Mridula sitting in her room that late.

"What are you doing here at this hour? Shouldn't you be sleeping by now? Chavi has school tomorrow."

"I have to ask you something."

"What is it? Tell me."

"I will come straight to the point. Who was that man in the restaurant?"

"Who? I don't know whom you are talking about.", Seema avoided eye contact with her and started folding her clothes.

"Mummy don't deflect the question. You know what I am referring to. How you were checking him out and he too was looking at you admiringly."

"Rubbish! Don't cook up stories Mridula."

"Are you telling me, or should I ask Apoorva about it?"

"Appu doesn't know him.", she immediately regretted after blurting it out.

"Doesn't know whom? I knew some hanky-panky was going on there."

Seema had turned red by now. She started fumbling and stuttering. Mridula came near her and held her hand tightly, "You can confide in me. Don't worry, I will not tell Apoorva if you don't want me to."

"You will not let it go, will you?"

"No, now tell me."

"Ok then. His name is Nishant. He was my class fellow in school."

"Really? How do you remember him and on top of that, how did you even recognise him after such a long time? It must be, what, four decades?"

"How can I forget him? We were very good friends. He wanted to marry me."

"Interesting! Go on, tell me more."

Seema was relaxed now and started telling Mridula in detail.

"He came to meet my parents, to ask my hand in marriage, but they did not agree to our match, as he was from a different caste. He tried contacting me after my marriage, but I did not entertain him. He took a house near our place so that he could see me at least once in a while, whenever our paths crossed. You see staying near made it more probable to meet in the market, restaurants or any other such public place."

"How romantic. How peachy!", said Mridula, placing her hand on her heart and giving Seema a wide smile. "Papa didn't know about him? Who all are there in his family? Have you guys ever spoken?"

"Take a breath. One question at a time."

"Wait, I think Chavi is calling me. I will go, put her to sleep, we will continue tomorrow."

"Ok. Good night."

Next morning, Mridula started the conversation again at the breakfast table.

"Yes mummy, tell me about his family."

"You were just waiting to be alone with me!", Seema said coyly. She continued from where she had left at night, "His wife expired some four-five years back."

"How do you know? Do you guys talk?"

"Once in a while when no one is accompanying us.", informed Seema giggling. "He has a daughter and a son. Daughter stays in Mumbai after marriage and son is a citizen of Canada. Yesterday he had come with his daughter's family to the restaurant. She must be visiting him. Otherwise, he lives alone with a servant."

"Hats off to you, for carrying on like this, without papa's or Apoorva's knowledge."

"You are not completely right there. Apoorva knows that my class fellow lives nearby. He also has a hint that he was interested in me. But he doesn't know the whole story which you now know."

"Mummy.... I was thinking.... why don't you meet him properly, like meet openly and talk. You can call him over or go to his place."

"What are you talking? How is it possible?"

"And why not? He is alone, you too are ..., you know what I mean."

"What will people say? What will Apoorva think?"

"Stop worrying about people. Who are these people anyway? And you two would meet like any other acquaintance. What is wrong in that? As far as Apoorva is concerned, I will talk to him. I am sure he will have no objections to it."

CHAPTER ELEVEN

Summer of 2009

New Delhi

It was very hot that evening. Seema, Nishant, Apoorva, Mridula and Chavi were sitting in the drawing room enjoying cold coffee with ice cream. Mridula had never seen her mother-in-law so happy before as she was appearing those days. She was glad that she took the decision of uniting old friends.

Nishant was narrating his trip to Niagra Falls in Canada, when he last visited his son there. In the midst of this nattering, Apoorva's phone rang. He checked it, picked it up and went outside the room to take the call. Mridula was observing his body language, she sensed something odd in his behaviour and the way he talked into the phone. He was literally whispering into the phone, which meant that it was not an official call, in addition to that, he went out into the garden, which meant he wanted privacy. Mridula's radar had picked up a fishy conduct.

Next morning when Apoorva was in the bathroom, she opened his phone to browse through it. She started checking call history, then messages and then went to his mails. She found nothing suspicious, all seemed normal. She was not convinced. Her hunch was telling her something different than what was appearing as she did not find any call record, at the time he had gone out to receive the call.

***

A few days later

Mridula was in the kitchen preparing dinner for everyone. Chavi was with Seema, who was having her recite counting and correcting her whenever she made a mistake. While Mridula was rolling chapatis, she heard a faint laugh. After a while she heard a giggle. She stopped to observe where it was coming from. It was coming from the kitchen garden. She thought it was Ravi who had gone to his room to do some work. She peeped out from the window, intending to scold him for not returning to the kitchen, but was startled to see Apoorva instead, busy on the phone. Her suspicion was aroused once again.

She closed kitchen's exhaust fan and placed her ear on the door which opened into the kitchen garden, to hear more clearly.

"Yeah, you like that? Sure.... why not? I will give you tomorrow...... I don't know, you will come, oohhh...... now you will say that? I will only give it in person. I told you, I am only free at the lunch time. That's good. Ha ha ha......", Apoorva was wheedling into the phone.

Her hand went to her head to stop the sudden giddiness she felt. She smelt something suspicious in the way he was talking. She had to be certain about this.

After dinner when Apoorva went to wash hands, Mridula quickly opened his phone and checked the last dialled number. Her gut feeling was right.

***

Next day

As usual, Mridula took Chavi to board the school bus in the morning. Apoorva left for office. Mridula got lunch ready for Seema. She left the house on the pretext of going to the parlour at about half an hour past noon. She was headed instead to the block of Lawyer's chambers at the Delhi High Court. The lunch break of the high court was from 1:15PM to 2:15PM. She calculated the time and expected to reach there around 1:30PM. She had packed lunch for two people, as she needed some excuse to go to his office.

She got down the taxi and proceeded straight towards Apoorva's office. She asked a couple of people about the directions and at about 1:40PM was standing outside his office door. Taking a deep breath, she opened the door.

There she saw a tall, fair and a beautiful lady, in a blue denim and a red top, sitting on her husband's table, right opposite him. Her legs were shaky as she walked towards them. They didn't notice her enter as they were busy talking and Apoorva was showing her something in the mobile.

"Surprise!", said Mridula when Apoorva lifted his head from the phone.

"You? How come you are here? I mean is everything okay at home? What brings you here?", blurted out Apoorva simultaneously pulling back his mobile towards him.

"I got you Lunch. Won't you introduce me to your companion here?"

His mouth was completely dry, he struggled to find words, "She is my client, she is my.... my wife."

"Whose name I guess I know.", snarled Mridula. She saw a shopping bag in her lap, from which a new, tagged, expensive leather purse was peeking. "So, this is what he has gifted her.", she thought.

"Won't you show me the purse he has gifted you, Shefali?", she asked the female directly.

Dumbfounded, she kept looking at Mridula, who in turn kept the tiffin on the table and turned and exited the office. Her heart was throbbing loudly, she kept her hand on the chest and took deep breaths to calm herself down.

In the evening, Mridula confronted Apoorva regarding Shefali. Initially they had a face off which slowly converted into a fight.

"When I can't trust you, how do you expect me to behave normally with you?"

"It's not a big deal. Don't make a mountain out of a mole hole. What is wrong if I gifted something to my client?"

"Ex-client! You promised to stay away from her. Had I done the same, how would you feel? Tell me."

"Go do it. Why would I stop you from gifting anyone, anything?"

"It's not just a gift Apoorva. You are acting very innocent, unnecessarily. I am not a kid to not make two plus two equals four. How does your conscious allow you to do this? Otherwise, you are very sensitive, why don't you understand my feelings here?"

"Don't eat my head for a small issue."

"Small issue? I don't know what's going on between you two. Why do you only gift her and not your other clients?"

"Stop it! Enough! Don't annoy me or you will regret it.", he, pointed a finger at her and raised his voice.

She felt so helpless. It all seemed so unfair to her. Not only was she physically weaker than him, but she also had no one in the house who would understand and support her, the fact was, she felt alone in his house.

Mridula, along with Chavi, shifted to the guest room, after that fight. She maintained her distance from Apoorva. They only conversed when mundane matters so required. Apoorva tried to persuade her to let go of inconsequential matters and restore normalcy for Chavi's sake, but she remained adamant and steadfast in her decision.

CHAPTER TWELVE

Autumn of 2009

New Delhi

Mridula was in the kitchen, making Mathris, when a message flashed on her phone. She continued her work. The message flashed again and then again. Curious, she checked it. It was from Sumit. He was coming to Delhi for 15 days. Her eyes widened; she was as happy as a dog with two tails. She hesitated for a moment then messaged back, "We have to meet. Send me your complete itinerary."

Sumit messaged back, "Can't wait to see you."

***

A few days later

For once in her life, Mridula wanted to be led by her heart and not her brain. She wanted to take a blind leap, keeping faith in the higher powers. "Nothing is random in the world. Behind every existence and every happening, there operates an invisible hand working for a larger purpose, which we may not recognise at the time, but it perfectly fits like a thread in the tapestry of life.", she recalled Sumit's words.

Her Choosing Apoorva over Sumit, meeting with Sumit when she went to stay with her parents, Sumit coming to Delhi, all these events were not planned by her. They were simply happening, with very little choice or planning on her part. She felt that certain things are just meant to be.

She also believed that there is a mysterious force which links one event to the other in a chain of life. Nothing is coincidence. There are events which require us to take a decision. Our decision paves the path of our journey to our destination. So, our destination doesn't depend on any chance or is not predestined, it is essentially chosen by us for which we cannot and should not blame anyone else.

She trusted God and went to see Sumit. She felt broken and cheated. She needed someone to unburden herself. Someone who would have understood her; with whom she could open her heart; who would tell her that whatever she was feeling and going through was unjust. That person, who would have guided her impartially, was none other than Sumit.

***

A week later

Mridula was lying next to Sumit, in a bed of the hotel room where he was staying in Delhi. This was their fourth meeting since he had come to Delhi, which had ended up in copulation. She felt that mating him was although enjoyable, but it was neither fulfilling nor satisfying, as it was with Apoorva. With Sumit,it was more of a bodily hunger, rage and resentment over her relationship with Apoorva. She was hurt and frustrated with Apoorva's behaviour. She was unable to get through to him with how disappointed and betrayed she felt. She had hoped for a contended and fulfilling life with her husband. Instead, here she was.

She had shared her feelings with Sumit, who understood her and sympathised with her. She cried in helplessness in front of him. He hugged her to console her. And in a weak moment they consummated their relationship. She was astonished as she did not feel any guilt or shame afterwards. Infact, she met him three more times, fully prepared and willing for fornication.

He had to return back to Indore the next day. They both wanted to spend more time with each other, but she had to go back to her house, as she could not be absent from there for a long time.

"I better be moving. It's quite late already.", she broke the silence.

"Stay for ten minutes more."

"Sumit, I want to tell you something. All this... whatever happened between us during the past few days, was beautiful, but..."

"But....", he dreaded about what she would say next.

"It can't happen again. I mean don't expect any commitment from my side."

"If it was beautiful then why can't it happen again?"

"Because I have a family. I don't want to leave my family. I don't want to be unfair to you too. Don't want to keep you in a lurch."

"I understand that much that you have a family. But why can't it happen again?"

"Let me be very honest. This thing which we have, cannot go on for long. It was a weak moment but a beautiful one.", she paused then resumed, "Yet a weak moment only. My commitment to my marriage is hundred percent although currently I am extremely upset with Apoorva."

"That's not fair."

"What do you expect from me then? I should leave him or continue on two boats? I am sorry, either is not possible for me. I wish, things were a bit different. I wish, I wish, in next birth, they are different."

"I am befuddled. I don't understand what you are saying. Doesn't make any sense to me."

"It all will make sense once you think from my point of view. We will be in touch, but this is not ......let me rephrase it, I can't pull it off."

She turned towards him, kissed him passionately and whispered, "Thank you for making me smile, for understanding me. Thank you for everything." Her heart broke when she left his side to dress up. She opened the door, waved at him and left.

***

After a month

New Delhi

Evenings were getting chillier as the winters were approaching. Mridula was making Atta Halwa for Chavi in the kitchen; Chavi was watching TV in the drawing room with her dad, Seema was busy over the phone. Mridula's phone rang.

"Hello Varsha, my dear! I was thinking of calling you. How are you?

"Yeah, I know! Then you didn't find time, isn't it?"

"Don't mock me. I was seriously going to call you. Anyway, tell me how is your son? What about your hubby dear?"

"They both are good. Rajiv is very busy in setting up his new office, so he comes back late now a days."

"Hmmm......, and what else is going on in your life?"

"All the usual stuff. Yeah, planning to put Aarav in play school. He needs some discipline in life, and I need some breather."

"Sure, a temporary relief it will be!"

"Have you guys become normal now or still your drama is continuing?"

"What normal, I don't think the things will ever be back to the way they were earlier. It's fine by me. I have become used to it. But now I have a new tension."

"Now what?"

"I have skipped my periods. I am scared that I might be pregnant."

"Wow! Congratulations dear."

"You don't understand. I and Apoorva have not slept together in a long time....."

"Oh! So do you think it could be ......how could you be so careless Mridu?", Varsha was concerned.

"Yes! And that is why I am quite disturbed because of it."

"Alright! First of all, don't trouble yourself at the moment till you are not sure about the pregnancy. And even if you are pregnant, he doesn't have any face to tell you anything when he himself is not very straight, isn't it? Is he making any efforts in this relationship? Does he even realise what wrong he has done to you? He, in his arrogance, didn't even stop you from shifting to the other room."

"Easier said than done. But yeah, you are right, I should try to calm myself down. Have to face whatever is in store for me, right?"

"Right! Do call up whenever you are feeling low. Don't just keep thinking and get worked up. I am always there to give you a hearing ear."

"I know, and I am thankful to God for that."

CHAPTER THIRTEEN

Winters of 2009

New Delhi

Mridula was standing in front of the bathroom mirror, blankly looking at her reflection. The ground seemed to rip away from beneath her feet. But she gathered herself, mustered the courage, and made up her mind to tell him that very evening.

*****

Next day, morning

Apoorva was driving to office in heavy traffic. He was in an awful mood since last night. He was replaying in his head what Mridula had said to him when she came to his room. Like a cacophony of a broken musical instrument, it was making noise in his head and had created a bad headache. In his bafflement, he did not realise that the car ahead of him had stopped suddenly. By the time he could perceive what was happening, he had already hit the still car, damaging his car's bumper and the other car's boot.

It took him some time to come to his senses and realise what had just happened. He got down to assess the loss and apologised to the driver. The angry driver demanded money for his damages, which he had to shell out.

After reaching office, he had a glass of water, sat down and closed his eyes. He was unable to accept whatever Mridula had told him; how could anyone, who was in his shoes. His wife carrying another man's child, what disgrace, how despicable!

What had gone wrong? He thought about his own infidelity and flirtatious nature. Yes, they were not an ideal couple, but they were in love, at least he thought they were. He thought about Chavi.

His mind was racing. "I will not accept it. I will ask her to leave immediately. She can leave, I will take care of Chavi."

***

At night

Apoorva called Mridula to his room after Chavi had slept.

Mridula was explaining, "No matter what I do, I can't change whatever has happened. There is nothing perfect in this world. Neither people are ideal nor are their relationships. You have to accept your circumstances, compromise for the sake of loved ones and move on in life, this is what I have learnt with experience."

"I don't believe in compromises. I have never compromised in my life. Even when I fell in love with you, I was clear what I wanted and never compromised on it. You used to be different or at least I perceived you to be different, than what you have become now. Time has changed you, Mridula.", snarled Apoorva.

"No, not just time, circumstances change people. May be my wordings were wrong. I had to say adjust in life and not compromise. We cannot act so rigid in life and hope to be happy. The stiffest **tree** is most easily cracked, while the bamboo survives by bending with the wind.", said Mridula.

"No circumstance justifies this, this...."

"Whenever there is adultery, a man and a woman, both are involved. Why is it that the woman must take the brunt of it, both physically and socially. God has created biological laws and man has created social laws. Both are unfair towards the woman only. Not done!"

"Talking of unfair, all this is unfair towards me. You sleeping around like a whore and expecting me to accept this child? You leave Chavi with me and go to your parents. I don't want to be with you."

She had tried her best already, she had nothing to add, so she quietly went out of the room. That night she wept and wept and finally made up her mind.

***

Next morning

The clock was showing 7:15AM. It was a calm morning after yesterday night's altercation between Apoorva and Mridula. Ravi was in the kitchen preparing morning tea. He was surprised that Mridula had not come to the kitchen yet, who would otherwise enter the kitchen before 7AM to prepare Chavi's lunch box. He thought of taking her tea to her room in case she overslept and lest little Chavi would miss her school bus.

Ravi came running to Seema's room and barged inside without knocking, "Maaji, Maaji...something has happened to bhabhi......please come quickly."

Seema hurried to Mridula's room, which was six-seven yards away from hers.

Seema tried to wake her up by shaking her vigorously. Mridula seemed to be in deep sleep and just made some squeaks in response. Seema shouted out loud to call Apporva from upstairs, "Appu! Come down immediately, fast!"

Everybody was in Mridula's room trying frantically to wake her up. Her eyes were shut, and she barely mumbled a couple of times, incoherently.

"Ravi, give me a hand, we have to take her to the hospital.", instructed Apoorva, trying to lift her up in his arms.

"I think she has taken my sleeping pills. I don't understand what is going on between the two of you. This is no way.", muttered Seema under her breath.

"Not now, this is not the time for all this. You can do it later, after I bring her back from the hospital safely.", commented Apoorva.

Chavi was standing in the doorway confused. She came inside and hugged Seema, who took her in her arms to comfort.

Apoorva was blabbering while driving the car, "You can't do this. How could you? Didn't you think about me? Forget about me, what about Chavi? How much can I take?"

Mridula unconscious, stirred in the back seat. Apoorva was keeping one eye on her and the other on the road.

CHAPTER FOURTEEN

Summer of 2010

New Delhi

In her ninth month of pregnancy, Mridula tried to keep herself as active as possible. She tried to do as much household chores, as much as her health permitted her to. She went for evening walks with her mother-in-law to a park, near their house.

She was also searching for a job which she could take up after the baby's delivery. Apoorva had encouraged her to find a suitable job for herself, to keep her busy and find a let out from the boring mundane routine of the house.

Seema had come to know about her pregnancy after she came back from the hospital. Initially, she was very angry and was in a denial mode, where she stopped talking to her. But after a few days of mulling and considering everything; her family, Chavi, turmoil phase of their relationship, when Mridula must have taken that extreme step and specially after talking to Apoorva, she slowly accepted the unborn child, as her grandchild.

Apoorva had explained to Seema that he had adjusted to the fact and had accepted the unborn child as a gift from God, since none of it was it's fault. Moreover, if they rejected that child and asked her to terminate the pregnancy, it would be unfair to the unborn child and a sin in God's eye. If he did not accept the child and asked her to leave their home, then that meant that Mridula would have either left them leaving Chavi behind or would have taken Chavi along with her; either scenario would be unfair to Chavi. It was not Chavi's fault that she be raised without her mother or father's love. If she took Chavi with her then he would not be able to stay without his daughter. Somewhere he felt a little guilty too, as he had wronged Mridula, disregarded her emotions and had gone ahead with his affair with Shefali, in spite of her showing her displeasure clearly.

Apoorva had explained to Seema, "So, mom, the sooner you accept the situation and move forward, the better it is for all of us. And I definitely do not want to lose Mridula. I realised how much I love her and need her in my life, only after I almost lost her. When she had gone to her parents' house, I had some hope of seeing her again someday, her coming back to me one day. But that day, when I was taking her to the hospital, a realisation dawned on me. I realised the fragile nature of life. How we take it for granted, thinking that we are born immortals, with infinite time at our disposal. No, ...no, life doesn't work that way. Like we need to invest in an account, in order to make withdrawals, similarly, in life, we need to invest in love, give time and patience to the relationship, in order for it to flourish and enrich us in return. Life is nothing without healthy relations."

To this Seema had added, 'You are saying the right thing Beta. Also, mother nature has proven from time immemorial that only those species that have adapted to changing climates and circumstances have survived, rest have been wiped out. So, yeah, I agree that we must accept the coming child with open heart and arms. For the sake of our family, for the sake of whatever she has done for our family, for her as a woman who nurtures, I would like to forgive her and give her another chance. It will take time, I know, but all will be normal in time to come."

***

A month later

Mridula was feeling some discomfort after waking up in the morning. Considering it as the usual pregnancy uneasiness, she continued to do her work. Disregarding it as something not requiring her attention, she tried to take her mind away from it. But when she sat down to have her lunch, the discomfort was so intense that she had to immediately rush to the toilet. Seema sensed something was wrong and followed her.

"Is everything okay?", asked Seema from outside.

Mridula replied from the bathroom, "I think it's time to go to the hospital, my water broke."

"Okay, I will bring the hospital bag and call the taxi, you call up Apoorva and tell Ravi to take care of Chavi while we are at the hospital."

Mridula and Seema reached hospital. Soon enough Apoorva too joined them. Mridula was taken to the labour room. They both waited outside on a bench.

After a couple of hours, a nurse came out of the labour room to tell them that it would take time, if they wanted, they could have something to eat from the canteen.

Late night, another nurse came out of the labour room to inform them that they were blessed with a baby girl. Apporva smiled and said that they would be calling her 'Brinda', since she was as holy as basil.

Apoorva found some time alone with Mridula the next morning after the delivery. Chavi was in the nursery and Seema had gone home to get some rest.

"I know it is not the right time for this, but I wanted it off my chest. I understand that whatever has happened between us, we need to have a very clear understanding regarding our relationship moving forward. So just hear me out patiently."

"I am listening."

"I know it is difficult, but we must let go of the past baggage, cut each other some slack once and for all, and move forward into our new life on a positive note. Forgive each other, stop expecting the other person to run according to us and instead play a constructively supportive role in each other's life, if possible. We must do this, if we want a peaceful life for us and for our kids."

"It is very much possible. You are asking us to be together, yet a foot apart!"

"With dignity, trust, mutual respect and grace!"

CHAPTER FIFTEEN

Autumn of 2010

New Delhi

Rama had come to help Mridula to take care of both the daughters. She stayed for two months, ensuring that Mridula was strong enough to take care of her daughters and the house. She stayed with Mridula in her room, on the ground floor of the house. Seema had asked Apoorva and Mridula, not to disclose anything to Mridula's family about Brinda being born out of wedlock.

Rama was perceptive enough to sense the hidden tension in the atmosphere and inquired from Mridula, "Don't you think that your husband and mother-in-law are not very happy to have a second daughter? Perhaps they wanted to have a boy, especially your mother-in-law must be hoping for a boy, thinking your father-in-law would be reborn in his own house." Mridula was quick to reply, "You are unnecessarily over taxing your head. Nothing like that. Brinda is small and requires more of a mother's care. Plus, you are also here now to look after us. So, maybe because of that reason they don't come in this room that often."

***

As a six-month-old baby, Brinda was a very active and a happy go lucky child. 'Anna Prashan' function was celebrated at home to commemorate this occasion. Some neighbours, friends and Gaurav had come to celebrate the first solid feed to be given to her. Mridula prepared Sooji Kheer for the occasion.

Gaurav stayed back for a couple of days, to spend some more time with his little niece. He was delighted to hear that Mridula would be joining a good firm shortly after, which allowed her to work from home. She only needed to visit her office once in a week or so; that too if required. With advancing technology, it was becoming easier for working mothers to manage both house and work.

In the evening, Ravi had prepared tea for everyone. Mridula was nursing Brinda, in her room. Seema was in the garden with her teacup, overseeing Chavi playing on a swing, especially set up for her, over there. Apoorva was accompanying Gaurav in the drawing room for tea.

Gaurav spoke after taking a sip of his masala tea, "I am happy to see you both well-adjusted with each other."

"We are still in the process Gaurav, it's a long journey, still. We are good learners though."

"I totally understand. That is all what is required. To be open to listen to other's point of view and to speak out, what you feel inside; to not just keep accumulating hurts or judgements in one's head. Open conversations and little patience can save many misunderstandings. They say that behind every successful man, there is a supportive woman. It is equally true that behind every happy woman, there is an understanding man."

Apoorva pensively looked afar, "We have mutually agreed to give each other space."

"What exactly do you mean by that?"

"We have decided to be together since we are our unhappiest when we are apart. And that's a fact. Since staying together was suffocating at times, we decided to not to interfere in each other's affairs but at the same time support one another in whichever way we can. After all it's our family, who else can take our place or care for them better than us?"

"Okay, you want to be there for your mother and the girls, right? After all, I am sure you respect each other, for the commitment you have towards one another. It takes so much to create a family. One cannot spoil that for some momentary ego, in the process of life. Having said that, faith in a relationship can never be undermined. Husband and wife should be able to trust each other completely for the household to run smoothly and to tread fearlessly in life's journey. I hope you understand what I am saying."

"Yes Gaurav! Not only understand, but I also agree completely."

***

Autumn of 2012

Brinda was two years old and copied every action of her elder sister. Whole day she would toddle behind her, in the whole house. She wanted to do what Chavi was doing, she wanted to play with the same toy with which she would play. Sometimes when they fought, they brought the whole house down.

In the middle of one of their fights, Mridula tried to mediate and solve the issue.

Mridula to Brinda, "Betu, you can play with the ball while didi is playing with the drums. Go turn by turn."

Brinda talking in broken sentences to her mother, "Mine..., Brinda drummy...., didi bad....."

Mridula tried to explain to Chavi, "You are elder to her. You should give her what she wants. She will play for some time and will get bored, then you can play with it."

Chavi frowning, "She wants whatever I take, you should tell her, not me. You love her more, so you take her side.

Brinda is a bad girl, throw her out!"

Mridula scolding Chavi, "No Chavi, she is your sister. Never talk like that. You two should always play together, with love."

Seema entered the room, "What is all the ruckus about now?"

Mridula called Ravi, "Ravi! Take them to the park and play 'Catch ball' for some time. I will take care of the dinner."

After Ravi took the kids to the park, Seema commented, "Don't you think, now you should move upstairs with Apoorva?"

Mridula did not reply anything.

Seema continued, "It's been a long enough time in my opinion, for things to come back to normal."

"Appu will unnecessarily get disturbed with these two monkeys. He has his work and...."

Seema cut her short, "He can always work from his den, when he needs quiet."

"Den.... you mean study? Yeah of course!"

"I will speak to him too."

Epilogue

28th October 2019

New Delhi

It was a day after Diwali. Chavi and Brinda were playing in the garden. Ravi and Mridula were busy in the kitchen making arrangements for the evening. Nishant, his daughter and his grand children were coming for dinner. Seema was peeling peas in the drawing room. Apporva was sitting next to her, eating freshly peeled peas, on the pretext of helping her.

Mridula came out of kitchen and sat next to them. "Wow! Look at you, so busy helping mom!" They all laughed.

Mobile phone rang, Mridula realising it was her's, got up to take it.

"Hello! Yeah...yeah....almost complete. I will WattsApp you once it is finalised. Yes, I know, ... before midnight. Sure,....bye, bye."

Apoorva asked Mridula, "Your boss is again eating your head? Isn't it supposed to be a holiday for you?" He quickly realised that he should not push it, "Let me guide Ravi, you go and complete your work so that you can enjoy at dinner time with everyone."

Mridula puckering her lips towards Apoorva and playfully said, "Thank you honey! I owe you a big one."

In the late evening, the same day

After finishing dinner, everyone continued to sit around the dining table. Nishant observed that Mridula and Apoorva were engaged in a deep conversation with his daughter, Kanika. They found a common ground of interest in geopolitics. He enjoyed the discussion initially but five minutes into the conversation he felt lost. He excused himself to go and join Seema, who was sitting on a sofa, in the drawing room, observing Chavi narrating stories to Brinda and Kanika's kids.

"So how are you? It's been a while since we had a heart to heart."

"I am good apart from my knees, they are troubling me again. Thinking of showing to the orthopaedic, who sits near the shopping mall."

"So that is why I don't get to see you now a days in the park! I was wondering what was keeping you away from your evening walks."

"Also, Mridula had to go to the office all of last week. She had been coming back late in the evenings, so I had to takecare of the kids and the house. Otherwise, you know how it is—she usually manages everything herself. By the way I had come day before yesterday, on choti diwali, for about an hour but couldn't locate you."

"We went shopping to Connaught Place. Kanika wanted to pick up Knick knacks from Janpath, for gifting to friends."

"Okay! Her husband has not come this time with her. How are they getting along now? I hope they have left their differences behind and come to some mutual understanding for the good of the family."

"Yeah! They are still learning along the way."

"Differences are everywhere. Two siblings who have been raised by the same set of parents are also different; for that matter, even identical twins do not think alike, they too have their disagreements. Then how can we expect two individuals, who have been raised in two different homes, with different sets of morals and ideologies they grew up observing, to think alike and agree with each other, in every matter. There are bound to be misunderstandings."

"More so because of the expectations from the other person, whom you so dearly love, for whom you are ready to do anything.", added Nishant.

"Expectations are the root cause of disappointments; I agree, but aren't expectations natural between husband and wife? I mean from whom else would you expect?", Seema commented thinking about her son and daughter-in-law.

"Expectations will be there, but a rational mind should not be blocked in the process. One should try and put oneself in other's shoes, to understand their perspective too. Then only can there be true understanding of any given situation."

Seema replied immediately, "Could not agree more! Far-fetched ideas about an ideal relationship which does not exist anywhere, will not help. The whole concept of ideal relationship is from fantasyland. No two relationships are the same, they all have their own flaws and beauties. It is up to a couple to find their balance. They will find a balance provided there is a will to do so on both the sides."

"The process of finding a balance would be easier if young minds do not forget that when they themselves are not perfect, how can they expect the other person to be a perfect being. Everyone has weaknesses. "If one strives to be each other's strength, rather than focusing on the other's weaknesses for personal gain, the relationship can flourish, which in turn will enrich both individuals."

Seema was quiet now. Apoorva, Mridula and Kanika also joined them on the sofas. Ravi served ice cream to everyone.